Captain Cobwebb's Adv

Chloe Dunbar

This Armada book belongs to:

~~Helen~~ curtis

~~18 Blythwood Gardens~~

~~Stansted Essex~~

Also in Armada by Gordon Boshell

Captain Cobwebb
Captain Cobwebb's Cowboys
Captain Cobwebb's Cobra

More Captain Cobwebb titles will be published in Armada shortly

Captain Cobwebb's Adventurers

Gordon Boshell

Illustrated by Graham Thompson

Armada

First published in 1973 by
Macdonald & Co. (Publishers) Ltd.

This edition first published in
Armada in 1977 by Fontana Paperbacks,
14 St. James's Place,
London SW1A 1PF.

Printed in Great Britain
by Love & Malcomson Ltd.,
Brighton Road, Redhill,
Surrey.

CONTENTS

CHAPTER 1

THE THING FROM THE SKY

DAVID and Toby Green were trying to be good and there is no surer way of getting into trouble. If you just happen to be good, that's all right . . . it is when you start *trying* that things go wrong.

On this particular day the weather had turned very cold and wet and in the afternoon Mrs Green had said they must not play outdoors. Then Mr Green came home very early from his office and he sat by the fire and told them to be quiet because he wanted to think. (Whatever grown-ups do in their offices, it seems they always have to come home to think.)

So, since David and Toby couldn't go outside and be noisy – which is a natural thing for boys to be – and they couldn't stay in the house and be noisy, they felt rather frustrated until, just as they finished their tea, Mrs Green said: 'Now boys, remember your father wants to sit quietly and think. So do try to be good.'

Toby was just going to say 'How?' when David dug him in the ribs and said: 'I know! We'll clear the table for you, Mother.'

'Oh, how kind of you, boys,' said Mrs Green, surprised and very pleased.

'And we'll wash up all the things, too,' added David, 'and put them away for you.'

'So you can sit down by the fire and help Father to think,' said Toby. (He was sure that his brother had some exciting plan in mind.) 'Leave all the work to us.' And he began to load the dirty dishes on to the tea-trolley.

'Thank you, boys,' said Mrs Green and she sat down in an easy chair and took up her knitting and she looked across fondly at Mr Green and she said: 'Aren't they wonderful, Walter?'

'They are indeed,' answered Mr Green, 'and I shall think they are even more wonderful if they will load that trolley *quietly* and if they will move it *quietly* out of this room and if they will *quietly* close the door after them. And close the kitchen door *quietly*, too.'

'Oh, I'm sure they will,' said Mrs Green.

And they did.

'There! You see, Walter!' said Mrs Green.

'Mmmm,' said Mr Green, and he stretched his feet into the fireplace and toasted his toes. Then he leaned back and started to think and Mrs Green went on with her knitting.

After some time, Mr Green closed his eyes – probably so that he could think harder – and they sat quietly and peacefully in the firelight until at last Mr Green decided that he had thought hard for quite long enough and he opened one eye, then the other, and he looked across at Mrs Green and he said: 'You are smiling. What are you thinking of, my love?'

'I am thinking that before long I shall have no housework to do at all,' said Mrs Green. 'Tonight my boys keep me out of the kitchen and tomorrow I shall start using the new electric washing machine you so kindly bought me. Think of it – all the drudgery of washing-day banished for ever! You are so good to me, Walter.'

'No more so than you deserve, my dear,' said Mr Green, gallantly.

And it was at this happy moment that David and Toby came back into the room.

'All finished, boys?' asked Mrs Green.

'Oh, yes,' said Toby.

'Yes,' said David. 'But I'll tell you one thing,' he added, '— that new electric machine of yours isn't much good, is it? It smashed most of the cups and saucers before we could stop it.'

'And it didn't even get them clean, either,' said Toby. 'We had to wash the rest by hand – and *we* only broke a plate and the sugar-basin between us.'

'A machine?' said Mrs Green puzzled. 'A machine? But we haven't got . . .'

Mr Green must have stopped thinking altogether by this time because he jumped to his feet and he pulled at his hair wildly and he said, in a very loud voice indeed: 'Yes, we HAVE a machine . . . a machine for washing blankets and sheets and clothes! A brand-new machine! A very costly machine! And these young jackanapes have filled it with cups and saucers!

'Get them to bed!' Mr Green demanded. 'Get them out of my sight! I am going into the kitchen to examine this machine and if they have broken it they shall have no more pocket-money from now until . . . until . . . until DOOMSDAY!!' cried Mr Green as he ran from the room.

There was a silence. And then Toby, who has a mathematical mind, said: 'But he *can't* stop our pocket-money from now until Doomsday, because none of us will live that long.'

'And anyway,' added David, 'in another few years we shan't need pocket-money because when we leave school you're going to be a bank-manager and I'm going to be an astronaut.'

'Off you go to bed. Right away!' said Mrs Green. 'How could you be such bad boys?'

'I don't know,' said David, truthfully. 'We *tried* to be good.'

'Yes – and that's all you told us to do,' said Toby, '— just *try*.'

'That will do,' said Mrs Green sternly (although it was quite obvious that as far as she was concerned, it wouldn't do at all). 'Not another word! Off to bed, the pair of you!'

So upstairs they had to go, and when they were in their bunk-beds – David has the top bunk and Toby the lower one – Mrs Green tucked them in.

'What about supper?' asked Toby, who likes food very much and often even dreams about it.

'No supper,' said Mrs Green firmly. 'And don't let me hear another sound from the pair of you all night.' And she switched off the light and went downstairs.

There was silence in the bedroom for a long time – quite fifteen seconds – and then David grumbled:

'What use is a washing-machine if it won't wash things?'

'They should have called it a smashing-machine,' said Toby brightly, but David was too cross to laugh. 'It's *hours* before our proper bed-time,' he said, gloomily, 'and I'm hungry.'

'So am I,' said Toby. 'Would you like a sausage-roll?'

'Of course I would, silly ass, but we shan't get any supper, so what's the good of talking about sausage-rolls?'

'It's a lot of good,' replied Toby, 'because I've *got* some sausage-rolls. I always keep a few handy in case I get hungry in the night or in case the house catches fire.'

'You can't put a fire out with sausage-rolls!'

'No, but they'd be nice to eat while you were watching the firemen put it out.'

'All right, all right,' said David hastily. 'Where are these sausage-rolls and how many have you got?'

'I hid them in the toes of my wellington boots at the back of the wardrobe,' said Toby, 'and I think there are four left. So you can have two.'

He rolled out of his bunk and began to pull on his dressing-gown. Then suddenly, he cried out: 'David! David! Look at my hand! Look at yours! Is it the same?'

'Yes! Yes! It is! The little blue spot seems all lit up!'

And indeed a tiny blue light was shining at the bottom of the first finger on each boy's right hand and twinkling like a star.

And then Toby said another amazing thing.

'It must be Uncle Septimus Cobwebb!' he said.

'You know what to do, Toby!' David called. 'Both together . . . one, two, three . . . NOW!'

And each boy placed the little finger of his left hand over the shining blue spot and they said together:

'Please make an adventure for us, Uncle Septimus.'

They lifted their fingers. The tiny lights had gone out. There was a strange, eerie silence.

At last Toby said: 'I wonder what's going to . . . ?'

He never finished the sentence. For, at that moment, the house was buffeted by a great blast of wind.

The bedroom curtains billowed upwards until they flapped against the ceiling. The window was flung wide open. The boys scrambled on to the linen-chest beneath the window-sill and stared out into the night. And, as the white sheet-lightning flickered among the rolling clouds, they saw the strangest sight.

From a great hook in the wall of the house above the bedroom window a shining wire cable stretched out over the houses, the roads and the fields, sloping upwards until it vanished in the sky.

And hanging from this cable, and coming towards them at a terrific speed, was a sort of huge basket, propelled by wide, powerful wings, that flapped from each side of it.

'It'll come right through the window!' cried David. '*Duck*!'

And the two boys rolled off the chest and flopped flat on the floor of the bedroom as the mysterious winged basket, growing bigger and bigger as it approached, screeched down upon them!

CHAPTER 2

A FANTASTIC VISITOR

Now about the mysterious glowing spot on the boys' fingers and the equally mysterious Uncle Septimus.

Long ago, when the boys' uncle, Septimus Cobwebb, was a boy himself, he went out into a meadow where the fairies were supposed to dance and he left a note to his father saying he was going to sit in one of those dark green circles in the grass – the ones people call fairy rings – until the fairies appeared. Well, the fact is that Uncle Septimus Cobwebb never came home, not ever again. But one day Grandfather Cobwebb received a note from him which said that he was well and happy but he was not coming back and that if anybody in the family needed help they should get in touch with him by a certain secret method.

Mr Green did this one day when David and Toby were bored and wanted an adventure, and in no time at all they found themselves fighting off bloodthirsty pirates and discovering hidden treasure. Captain Cobwebb, as he now called himself, was so pleased with their bravery that he gave the boys a kind of private radio link with him, to use whenever they wanted another adventure. He made a little blue mark come at the bottom of the first finger of their right hands. He said that if they touched that mark with the little finger of the left hand and asked him for an adventure, one would start to happen straight away.

This time, as Toby had guessed, Uncle Septimus must have decided to call *them*, to remind them that there was no need to stay, hungry and bored, in a stuffy old bedroom. I'd have liked to tell you more about that adventure with the pirates but we haven't a moment to spare, because . . .

WHOOSH! The great flying basket reached the end of the cable . . . swung in through the window and up to the ceiling, flinging out something big and round like a great pumpkin. Then it fell back again to hang, with its huge wings folded flat against its sides, outside the window.

As the great round thing hit the ceiling the boys jumped to their feet and Toby quickly switched on the bedside lamp.

'When that thing hits the floor the bump'll bring Mother dashing upstairs,' said David anxiously. And at that, a strange voice seemed to come out of the air – a rich, round, fruity sort of voice.

'No so, laddie!' said the voice. 'Not by any manner of means, me young cock-sparrow! Observe closely . . .'

'Look . . . look!' cried Toby.

The big ball was shrinking rapidly as it fell – so rapidly that well before it touched the floor it was no larger than a table-tennis ball. It bounced lightly once or twice on the carpet without a sound.

And from the tiny ball there came, as the boys dashed forward, an equally tiny, but still very fruity, voice.

'There you are! Not a bump, not a whisper to disturb your mother and bring her hot-foot up the stairs. Stand back, me young friends, while I unshrink meself!'

The tiny ball began to rock violently from side to side and all the time it grew larger and larger – and the voice grew larger with it, making comments on its progress.

'Squeezed meself so small I nearly got the cramps . . . Aaahh! Oooh! Breathe deeply, me boy . . . that's better! Swelling up nicely now . . .!'

By this time the ball was about three feet high. And still it continued to grow.

'And now,' said the voice, 'permit me to reveal me noble features. In order, thus – ONE: me hat . . .' and from the top of the ball there suddenly shot up the crown of a very tall hat, like a very high and sooty chimney-pot, with a narrow brim beneath.

'TWO,' continued the voice, '— me noble brow . . .' (a wide forehead came into view). 'THREE: me large and lustrous eyes . . .' (The eyes were very *small*, in fact, but bright blue and sparkling, and they peeped out from under heavy lids).

'FOUR: me noble Roman nose . . .' (It certainly wasn't a *Roman* nose – it was round, very big and very red. In fact, it was like a large, red, rubber ball itself).

'FIVE: me large and generous mouth, giving forth joyousness and words of wisdom . . .' (Well, it certainly was a very *large* mouth).

'SIX: me firm, stern chin – or should I say chins? I haven't counted 'em lately, laddies . . .' (There were *two* chins, anyway – perhaps more, because they vanished behind a great red silk cravat, a huge bunch of material stuck with a large pearl-headed pin and crammed between the vast wings of a stiff collar).

David and Toby were staring in wonderment, with their mouths wide open.

'Well may you gaze in wide-eyed fascination!' went on the strange person. 'You behold a phenomenon that has brought astonishment to audiences throughout the civilised world. And now, to complete the manifestation . . .

'SEVEN: arms, EIGHT: legs.' (The arms were short and the newcomer's legs were long and thin, but his body was as round as a great barrel. His clothing seemed to be of some check material and he also wore a very low-cut red waistcoat – which looked like velvet – to match his tie.)

'Nine: me monocle . . .' (he fixed this in his left eye) '. . . and TEN: this costly gold-headed cane – the gift of a noble lady who shall remain nameless.' (Where the cane came from, David and Toby couldn't tell – he just seemed to draw it from his sleeve.)

'We now stand before you,' went on the stranger, now very tall indeed, 'complete and in our natural size.' He made a low bow and went on importantly:

'Master David Green . . . Master Toby Green! May I present meself – Archimedes Strretch, known world-wide as *The Indiarubber Man* or *The Boneless Wonder*! At your service, laddies. I am the bearer of a message from me noble patron, Captain Septimus Cobwebb.' And before the boys could acknowledge his greeting, he drew a piece of paper from his pocket.

'Attention!' he said importantly. 'Here is the message . . .' And he began to read:

> '3 shirts washed and ironed,
> 6 pairs socks washed and darned,
> Add amount owing on last bill.
> TOTAL ....'

Mr Strretch stopped suddenly and his cheeks went as red as his nose. He hastily turned the paper over, coughed and began again: 'Captain Cobwebb says "Are you prepared to see this adventure right through to the end and not turn back, whatever the dangers?" '

'Yes!' said David, promptly.

'Of course!' said Toby. 'But what have we got to *do*, Mr Strretch?'

'First of all, laddie, to pass a test of courage. After that a perilous task awaits you. You have to wrest the Golden Cactus from the evil hands of that villainous Baron, Black Walter . . .'

'What's the Golden Cactus?' cried Toby, jumping with excitement.

'And who's Black Walter?' demanded David.

The words were scarcely out of his mouth when there was a sudden clatter from outside the window and Mr Strretch went scrambling over the window-sill into the flying basket. Its great wings were flapping frantically and he had to hold on to the overhead cable with all his strength to keep it from moving off.

'Captain Cobwebb must need us urgently!' panted Mr Strretch. 'Quick! Step lively, me laddies! I can't hold her much longer . . .'

'But we can't come in pyjamas!' protested David, scrabbling about in the wardrobe.

'No time . . . WHOA, there! . . . for clothes! Get your dressing-gown . . . seize some shoes . . . but HURRY!'

So they grabbed what they could, flung the things into the basket and scrambled in after them.

Mr Strretch let go the wire and, to the swift beat of its powerful wings, the flying basket swept them all upwards and away into the darkness of the night.

CHAPTER 3

MR STRRETCH GOES INTO BATTLE

DAVID and Toby struggled into their dressing-gowns and whatever footwear they'd been able to snatch from the wardrobe. The wind buffeted them, the basket swayed, and Mr Strretch stood with arms wide apart, gripping its rim and peering ahead.

The two boys scrambled on to the narrow seat that ran round the inside of the basket and knelt one on either side of him. They could just about get their noses over the rim and though they stared and stared in the same direction as Mr Strretch was looking, they could see nothing – nothing, that is, except an occasional glimpse of ugly, rolling storm-clouds as they were lit up by sudden flashes of lightning.

'Is this going to be a long journey, Mr Strretch,' David asked.

'That depends, me sprightly lad,' said Mr Strretch. 'When you set out on an adventure anything may happen, you know.'

'Well, in case anything *does* happen,' said Toby quickly, '— I mean if we get separated, for instance – hadn't you better tell us *now* about where we're going to and about the Golden Cactus and Baron Whatsisname?'

'A wise precaution!' agreed Mr Strretch. 'Well, now, listen . . . Long ago, in the Great Saffron Desert of Tombolia, a famous explorer found a strange kind of cactus. The people of the desert told him that if he could keep the cactus alive for a hundred years it would bear three flowers . . .'

'That's a lot of trouble just to get three flowers!' said David.

'Ah-ha, me noble friend, not so fast!' warned Mr Strretch. It would be well *worth* the trouble – because these flowers would be of purest gold . . . something unknown before in the whole world and of fabulous value.'

'I think there's a catch in it, though,' said Toby. 'I mean the explorer probably wouldn't *live* a hundred years!'

'No more he did,' said Mr Strretch. 'But before he died he gave the cactus to the people of the poor village of Blumendorf where he was born. They have tended it ever since, hoping that it would flower and bring prosperity to them.

'Last week, after a hundred years, the cactus put out three buds. Yesterday the buds began to open. The petals, everyone saw, were of gleaming gold!

'And last night Black Walter, the robber Baron of Bunkulm, swept down on the happy village with his evil band and carried off the Golden Cactus. Nobody knows yet where he has gone with it.'

'*We'll* find him!' declared David. 'We'll track him down wherever he is, won't we, Toby?'

'Yes, and we'll take the Golden Cactus right back to the people it belongs to,' added Toby. 'Are we going to the village now?'

'We're going to Captain Cobwebb's headquarters, which are near the village,' said Mr Strretch. 'We're climbing up to cross a mountain ridge now and when we reach the top I hope this flying laundry-basket will still have strength enough to carry us over the forest and safely across Howling Valley to the meeting-place.'

'What's Howling Valley?' asked David.

'And what is it that howls?' said Toby.

'Don't ask me, pray do not ask me,' answered Mr Strretch with a shudder. 'I would not wish to strike terror into your young hearts. Wait until we are safely across – then, maybe, I will tell you.'

David shivered in a sudden blast of wind. 'It's getting very cold,' he said.

'A little hot wine would be very consoling,' said Mr Strretch. 'Likewise, or otherwise, a sizzling steak. Or failing that, a ham sandwich spiced with pickled gherkins. Or would you perchance, me bright boys, have in your pockets a simple piece of broken biscuit or a not-too-dry crust of bread?'

'No such luck!' David began, fumbling in the pocket of his dressing-gown. But Toby called out loudly in dismay: 'Oh! oh! OH! Help! My feet!'

'Frostbite!' cried Mr Strretch. 'Rub his toes with brandy – infallible remedy . . . if only we had some.'

'But it's not frostbite,' babbled Toby as David struggled to help him pull off his wellingtons. '. . . It's . . . it's . . .' (off came the boots with a strange sucking sound) '. . . it's . . .'

'I knew it, luckless laddie, I knew it!' spluttered Mr Strretch. 'Your toes have been pecked by the Scissor-beaked Snargles – I was afraid we might run into some around here. They eat *anything*.'

'It's not Snargles either – whatever *they* are – ' said Toby. 'It's *sausage-rolls*. When I grabbed my boots, David, I forgot I'd hidden those four sausage-rolls in the toes. I couldn't think why my feet felt so cramped until Mr Strretch talked about food.'

'Well, let's get rid of all this mess,' said David, turning the boots upside down and beginning to bang them on the edge of the flying basket.

'Horror of horrors! Hold off! Refrain! Desist!' cried Mr Strretch. 'In brief – stop it, laddie!'

'But they're all squashed to bits!' David objected. 'We couldn't possibly eat them.'

'But the Scissor-beaked Snargles *can*!' shouted Mr Strretch. 'Listen! They *are* . . . they *have* . . . and they're coming for another helping!'

And with a loud clashing of steely beaks, a black and flapping horde of huge birds swept up from below, catching and devouring the falling food, then surrounding and attacking the flying basket in their eagerness for more.

They clawed at the sides of the basket. Their razor-sharp beaks snipped whole pieces out of its rim as they pounced on every crumb their greedy yellow eyes could see.

It was then that Mr Strretch showed his mettle.

'Down, my comrades-in-arms! Down!' he yelled. 'I will engage this rapacious crew! In short – duck your nuts and leave this little lot to me.'

And as David and Toby crouched low in the basket and covered their heads, Mr Strretch leaped on to the seat, grabbed the rope with one hand to steady himself and, holding his gold-headed cane firmly in the other like a fencing foil, he lunged at the attackers.

'Have at thee, varlet,' panted Mr Strretch. 'Ha, saucy knave. Take that . . . and that . . . and that!' As Mr Strretch prodded them from the sky the squawking horde grew fewer and fewer.

At last only one remained – a great, powerful rogue, twice as big as any of its companions.

'One more to go!' exulted Mr Strretch, lashing out

High in the sky Mr Strretch fights off the Scissor-beaked Snargle—battling madly to seize even a crumb of squashy sausage-roll from the inside of Toby's wellingtons. David says he'll never understand why the birds should be so crazy about it. But Toby insists that, at that altitude, even squashy sausage-roll would be haute cuisine.

with his cane as it swept past him. It nearly escaped, but not quite: it got a smart blow right on its tail. In a furious rage the Snargle swung its head round, snapping madly and . . . *its powerful scissor beak sheared right through the cable from which the flying basket was suspended.*

The cable parted with a sound like gunfire. The Snargle vanished as though a giant hand had plucked it from the sky. Mr Strretch, with a triumphant cry of 'Victory is ours!' still on his lips, was flung backwards on top of David and Toby. The great but weary wings of the flying basket flapped furiously as they tried to take the strain. But they were unable to keep the basket in the air and, slowly at first, then faster and ever faster, it began to plummet towards the earth.

'Action stations!' Mr Strretch had managed to get to his feet again and helped the boys to scramble on to the seat.

'Look over the side,' he ordered. 'First man to spot a tree call out "TREES"! Then I'll get ready to drop. It should be quite safe from tree-height.'

'But what about us?' demanded Toby.

'We'd break our legs at least,' said David.

'Have no fear,' said Mr Strretch. 'Trust me, laddies. I will see that you land safely. Maybe not softly – but safely!'

Toby would have liked a good deal more explanation about how Mr Strretch proposed to manage this, but just at that moment David called out 'TREES! TREES!'

Almost at once Mr Strretch had flung an arm round each of the boys and he began to breathe in and breathe in and to swell and to swell . . .

His legs seemed to draw up into his body and his head sank down into it until, in a very short time, only his arms – which gripped the boys tightly to his sides – and his stove-pipe hat, showed outside the surface of the enormous round ball he had become.

Down, down, down they plunged . . . Then, suddenly, there was a great jolt. The basket struck something solid and was jerked away from under them.

'Hold your breath!' commanded Mr Strretch. 'Here we go!'

Down and down they went. Branches snapped beneath their weight . . . crash . . . crash . . . but slowed the speed at which they fell.

All the same, when they hit the ground – or rather, when Mr Strretch hit the ground, because he was holding them well above it – there was a terrific bump.

At that moment Mr Strretch let go of them, before his bounciness took him up in the air again.

David and Toby were flung among small bushes and deep grass. The wind was knocked out of them and they lay for a few minutes getting their breath back before they managed at last to crawl to their feet.

'Where's Mr Strretch?' said Toby anxiously.

'Sssh! Listen!' said David.

The silence of the forest was broken by a strange sound. Loud at first, it was repeated again and again, at shorter and shorter intervals, growing softer and softer until it faded away into utter silence . . .

BUMP . . . BUMP . . . BUMP . . . Bump . . . bump . . . bump . . . bump bump bump *bump bump bump* . . .

Mr Strretch was *still* bouncing. Bouncing away from them, farther and farther and farther away . . .

And David and Toby were left to face the hidden dangers of the forest night alone.

CHAPTER 4

THE TERROR OF HOWLING VALLEY

By now the silence was complete. The air was warm – even to two boys dressed only in pyjamas and dressing-gowns – but in spite of this they shivered. Secretly they were scared.

But David didn't want to show he was frightened in front of his younger brother (since he was older, he felt he had to look after Toby). As for Toby, well, he wanted to show David that he was as brave as *he* was, if you follow me.

So they huddled there, beside a large bush in the long grass, and each waited for the other to speak.

At last David tried to give a little laugh. It was an effort but he managed it. 'Happy landings!' he said. 'That was very clever of Mr Strretch!'

'Yes,' agreed Toby. But he couldn't help adding: 'I wonder where he is now? D'you think we'll ever see him again?'

'Of course we will,' said David, bravely, 'because we'll go and look for him.'

'But we don't know where to look.'

'Yes, we do,' said David. 'We heard him go bouncing away in that direction. Look, Toby, the moon's coming out. We'll be able to see our way. I'll bet he bounced right along that sort of track between the big trees there. So we'll rest for a while and then we'll set off after him.'

Toby felt a bit more cheerful at this. He said: 'Perhaps he'll be having a rest like we are and then he'll come back along the track to look for us.'

'I'm sure he will,' said David.

'I bet he's hungry,' Toby said. '*I* am. Are you?'

'Famished. I could do with some eggs and bacon . . .'

'Or spaghetti *Bolognese* . . .'

'Or steak . . .'

'And chips . . .'

But David could not bear to think any more about his favourite dishes.

'Oh, shut up. Forget it!' he said.

'What! Forget about *food*?!' demanded Toby, indignantly.

David suddenly gripped his arm tightly and said 'Sssssshh!'

They held their breath and listened fearfully. The clouds had cleared completely now and the great white moon lit up the forest clearings with an uncanny light.

And then they heard it. Slight at first, the strange rustling grew until it was all around them, in the trees, in the deep grass, among the shrubs where they sat. Grasses bent and swayed, the leaves on the shrubs twisted and turned, tree branches quivered.

Suddenly Toby said: 'Look! Look at this bush, David. You can actually see it growing!'

And he was right. As the leaves turned and shook, a little bud appeared at the end of each branch. The buds grew and grew and then opened into huge white flowers . . .

'It must be something in the moonlight that makes them grow like this,' whispered David.

Whatever it was, it worked very quickly.

As they watched, the flowers died. The petals fell off and in their place a large white fruit began to grow . . . bigger . . . and bigger. And suddenly —

SQUELCH! One of the fruit burst open, shooting a great jet of milky fluid right into Toby's face! And as he fell back, gasping with the shock, the juice ran down his cheek and into his open mouth.

He looked so funny that David burst out laughing, but Toby leaped to his feet. He grabbed David by the sleeve.

'Quick! Quick!' he cried. 'Pull some of these off before they burst!'

David didn't ask any questions. He knew that there was only one thing that could make Toby so excited – FOOD. Together they pranced around the strange bush, pulling off as many fruits as they could before these were ready to burst – and dodging the jets of juice from those that did.

They took their prizes and sat some distance away in an open patch of grass. They stuck their fingers through the thin skins of the fruit and they drank and drank and drank . . . while all around them in the forest there was the *squish* . . . *squish* of the strange fruits as they burst. Little furry creatures moved amongst the undergrowth or came scurrying down the trunks of the tall trees and the boys could hear them – in their thousands, it seemed . . . lapping away.

'If it's good for them, it can't harm us,' said Toby,

starting on his fourth juicy fruit. 'Doesn't it taste super! It's like a wonderful mixture of spaghetti . . . and custard . . . and baked beans . . . and strawberry ice-cream . . . and . . .'

'. . . and onion soup . . . and treacle . . .' said David. '. . . and Frankfurters . . . and lemon-jelly . . .'

The forest fell silent again, for the moon's light was now waning.

Toby wiped his lips and he rubbed his stomach and he sighed blissfully.

'David,' he said sleepily, 'isn't it quiet and peaceful here!'

'Isn't it!' said David, yawning.

But they were both wrong. For just at that moment there broke out the most frightful and hideous howling that you could ever imagine. It rose and fell, it echoed and re-echoed through the forest. It seemed to be all round them.

'What is it, David?' whispered Toby, as they huddled together.

'I don't know,' said David, 'but I think we must be near that place Mr Strretch called Howling Valley.'

'He said he wouldn't tell us about it because he didn't want to terrify us,' said Toby. 'What do you suppose it is that lives in Howling Valley?'

'I don't know,' David said, and he added (trying to keep his teeth from chattering): 'Probably something that just likes to sit there and howl – and howling won't hurt *us*. Let's sit quietly where we are and wait until daylight.'

It seemed the only thing to do. So they sat and they sat but they didn't dare to close their eyes. The blood-curdling howls went on and on for a long time. Suddenly they stopped.

'Thank goodness for that!' muttered David.

But what followed then was more terrifying than the howling. First they heard a low, rumbling growl, far down the track between the trees. Then there was the soft pad . . . pad . . . pad . . . of something weaving through the undergrowth and coming nearer . . . nearer . . .

'Lie down flat and keep your head down,' whispered David, and he flung an arm round Toby as they both pressed their faces to the ground.

The pad . . . pad . . . of the creature faded away for a while, then they heard it again. This time it was behind them. Close . . . but still behind them.

Toby whispered: 'I think it's going away.'

But as he spoke there came from right above their heads a thunderous growl. Their hair rose and their necks tingled at the hot breath of the unseen creature as its fangs met in the necks of their dressing-gowns.

Pinned together, they were lifted effortlessly into the air. They could not raise their heads to see the muzzle of the monster that held them but, many feet below, they could make out two great hairy feet armed with massive deadly claws.

For a moment the huge beast stood pondering. Then, with a quick toss of its head, it plunged through the forest with a long, loping stride, carrying the two helpless boys towards its distant lair.

CHAPTER 5

AN EGG FOR THE OOOKUK

As for Mr Strretch, with his long experience of being an Indiarubber Man, or Boneless Wonder, he knew a good deal about bouncing. But he had never before made a bounce with a boy tucked under each arm and the extra weight had brought him down at such a speed that his first bounce – after he had released David and Toby – sent him even higher in the air than the point from which he fell.

What's more, the hefty bump shook him so much that it was a long time before he could even begin to shrink himself and so he bounced and bounced and bounced and bounced farther away from the place where he had let go of the two boys.

But at last he came out of his daze and he managed to make himself smaller and smaller, and his bouncing became less and less high and *much* quieter, because he was now just about down to the size of a golf ball.

Very cautiously Mr Strretch poked out his head for a quick glimpse around. The clouds were just clearing from the face of the moon. The forest seemed perfectly still. There was no sign of any wild beast. Just one small sound broke the silence as Mr Strretch prepared to land. It came from a little way off, and you or I would call it a rather pleasant sound. Like a bird call, in fact.

'Ooo . . . *kuk*! Ooo . . . *kuk*! Ooo . . . *kuk*!'

But Mr Strretch didn't think it was pleasant.

'Oh me! Oh my! Oh, calamity!' bleated Mr Strretch.

'Ooo . . . *kuk*!,' cooed the strange voice. And then, coming closer, 'Ooo . . . *kuk*! Ooo . . . *kuk*!'

'It's coming! Help!' Mr Strretch drew in his hat, and his head, and his arms and tried to make himself as small as possible. The last thing he saw, before he landed in the grass, was a winged and ghost-like thing flitting silently through the trees towards him.

'Oh, my! It *is* the Oookuk!' gasped Mr Strretch, and as fast as he could he rolled himself under the leaves of a plant that was something like a large primrose.

'Safe at last!' he breathed, while up above, the Oookuk, baffled by his sudden disappearance, flew around in circles uttering its plaintive cry.

If you knew as much about Oookuks as Mr Strretch knew, you'd be just as worried as he was about what could happen to him. But as this creature is mentioned only in very rare and learned books that you may not have read yet, I'd better tell you about it.

It's really an obstinate kind of cuckoo – it absolutely refuses to do anything in the same way that other cuckoos do. it won't say 'Cuckoo', – only 'Ooo-kuk' – and, in fact, if any ordinary cuckoo politely says to it, 'Good Morning. Nice Day,' the Oookuk will almost certainly reply gruffly: '*Nasty* evening. *Awful* night.'

But the thing about the Oookuk that frightened Mr Strretch so much is what it does about *eggs*. You see, ordinary decent cuckoos lay their eggs in other birds' nests. But the Oookuk, for a start, refuses to lay eggs at all – just because other cuckoos *do* lay them. And it goes and builds a nest of its own, just because ordinary cuckoos *don't*. And then it hunts around, collecting *other* birds' eggs . . . from an eagle's nest on the top of a cliff, or from the clumsy nest of a Scissor-beaked Snargle amid the thorns of the Birgl bushes, or even from the ground-level home of the Shylark* amongst the grass . . . and it takes them back to its *own* nest and hatches them *itself*. The Oookuk really is a most perverse creature.

This particular Oookuk had just finished building its nest and it was looking for the first egg to put in it when it caught a glimpse of a lovely little one – just like a Shylark egg – down on the floor of the forest.

It was only a glimpse, then the egg vanished from sight (as Mr Strretch rolled under the primrose leaf) but the Oookuk got so excited about it that it flew round and round over the spot, determined to find that egg.

Mr Strretch shivered with fright in his hiding place as he heard its puzzled cries, but he didn't dare to move and at last the Oookuk began to get weary (and a bit dizzy, too). It would most likely have gone egg-hunting somewhere else only . . . something strange started happening down below.

The first that Mr Strretch knew about this new danger was a faint quivering of the earth under him. Then a kind of scrabbling. Then a sort of snuffling.

And then . . . the ground beneath him began to shake violently. Then the soil began to boil up – just like milk boils up in a saucepan when you stop looking at it – and the next moment Mr Strretch was lifted up and up, right on the peak of a sort of volcano of earth. Up through the grass, up through the covering leaves he came. He looked like a little golf-ball on the tip of an enormous tee.

'Oh, oh!' gasped Mr Strretch. 'I'm on top of a mole-hill!'

* Shylark: – This bird is smaller than the common, rather noisy Skylark. It is very timid and blushes when spoken to.

'Ooo . . . ooo . . . ooo . . . KUK!' cried the delighted Oookuk. And with one swift swoop it grabbed Mr Strretch in one claw and carried him off in triumph to its nest amid the topmost branches of the tallest tree in the forest.

There it placed its treasure lovingly in the middle of the nest. Then, with an 'Ooo . . . *kuk-kuk-kuk*!' of joy, it fluffed out its warm breast feathers over Mr Strretch *and settled down to wait for its first egg to hatch*!

CHAPTER 6

IN THE GREAT BEAST'S LAIR

THE great beast that was carrying David and Toby weaved its way among the trees, making steadily towards the valley.

The two boys had not dared to speak to one another so far, in case their voices angered the creature. But when the animal suddenly began to shoulder its way noisily through a clump of tall bushes, David felt it was safe to talk and he said:

'Toby, listen! I know how you can escape.'

'Without you? Don't be a chump. I won't.'

'It's the only way. You must get away and find Mr Strretch. He knows all about Howling Valley and the things that live there and he'll know how to rescue me, if anybody does. But unless one of us gets to him how's he to know what's happened?'

Well, this seemed a very sound argument but Toby didn't relish the idea of leaving his brother in the hands – sorry, paws – of the beast.

'Suppose you get eaten?' he said.

'Of course I won't. *You're* going to rescue me. Why,' said David, clinching the argument, 'I rely on you, Toby!'

'Oh, all right then,' Toby said, really quite flattered. 'Tell me how we manage this escape.' And David quickly outlined his plan.

Now Toby was wearing his wellingtons, which are very difficult to remove, especially when your feet are all sticky with squashed sausage-roll and you are hanging far above the ground from the paws of a great beast. But David had managed to grab only his slippers before they scrambled into the flying basket and for him it was easy to slip one off, as the beast came out into the open again, and jerk it smartly far away to one side.

The sudden sound of its fall brought the beast to a halt. It turned its head and listened intently. David had hoped (it was part of his plan, in fact) that it would put them down and go to investigate. But after a moment it set off again.

There were now boulders and outcrops of rock among the grass. David took off his other slipper.

'Last chance!' he muttered and flung it sideways as hard as he could. It must have fallen on a boulder for there was a sudden sharp crack and then a slithering sound . . .

The great beast halted suddenly. It lowered the boys to the ground with a warning growl and sprang in the direction of the sound.

'Quickly, Toby!' whispered David. 'Slip your arms out of your dressing-gown sleeves and lie still. Sure you unfastened the cord? O.K. Now for it. Good luck – and see you soon!'

'See you soon,' answered Toby, though now the moment of his escape had come he had a nasty sinking feeling in his stomach.

The great beast came padding back. It stood over them and, with another growl of warning to them not to move, it gripped their clothing again, lifted its head and set off once more down the slope for Howling Valley.

But this time one of the dressing-gowns was empty and beneath the other David hugged a big stone so that the beast should not feel the difference in weight.

And behind the creature and its prey, Toby lay, motionless and hardly daring to breathe, until the sound of the beast's passage had died away.

Then, a small, lone figure in his pyjamas and wellington

boots, he set off towards the spot where they had last seen Mr Strretch bouncing away from them.

David, hugging the heavy stone, was most uncomfortable especially when, in the grey light of dawn, the beast began to go down a steep and rocky path. The weight of the stone made David swing about like a pendulum and this must have caused the beast some discomfort for it gave a sudden growl and shook its head angrily.

The first thing that happened as a result was that Toby's dressing-gown slipped from between its teeth and the second thing was that David let go the stone he was holding. The stone fell on the dressing-gown and carried it over the edge of the track so that it went flying, with the sleeves outstretched, down the steep, rocky slope. It looked just like a human body falling. The great beast dropped David on the path and lowered its head, moving it from side to side as it watched the fluttering dressing-gown plunge out of sight. And David. glancing cautiously upwards, got his first full view of the animal.

It was as big as . . . a . . . a *cow*. But it wasn't a cow. There was no doubt at all in David's mind about what it was. It was a *dog* – a great, enormous Shaggy Dog, with hair all over its eyes.

As David looked at it the dog lifted its head and howled until an answering howl came from far down in the valley.

Then the dog gave a series of sharp barks. And as it did so, David almost jumped out of his skin in amazement. Because . . . *when it barked he found he knew just what it was saying*!

'I'm coming home now,' barked the Shaggy Dog. 'Tell the pups I've got a People for them to play with. I caught two, but one fell down the ravine, so they'll have to share this one between them.'

With a wuff that was very much like a chuckle, the Shaggy Dog picked David up again and set off at a canter down the track. And David quite forgot his fears in trying to work out just how it was that he could actually understand what the Shaggy Dog had said.

He decided at length that, like many seemingly amazing things, it was really quite simple. You see, lots of people keep dogs and all those people will tell you if you ask them – and even if you don't – that their dogs understand every word they say to them. Well, then, if that's the case with people who own dogs, why shouldn't it be the case with dogs who own people?

And David thought also: 'My life's probably not in any danger at all! If dogs treat people like most people treat their dogs, this part of the adventure may turn out to be very pleasant and interesting indeed!'

The Shaggy Dog was loping along at a great speed now and they came to the bottom of the valley just as the sun rose. Cliffs rose high on either side, but in the valley there was grass and trees and a pleasant stream ran into a large and reedy lake. At the foot of the cliffs David could see the dark mouths of a number of caves. It was towards the nearest one that the Shaggy Dog was hurrying. It leaped the stream in one bound and loped up the grassy slope to the cave entrance.

There was a furious burst of yapping and all David's fears came back to him again as two fat, wriggly, shaggy animals as big as Shetland ponies came hurtling towards the Shaggy Dog.

'Put him down, Pop. Please put him down!' they yapped, jumping up at David.

'All right, then,' wuffed the Shaggy Dog. 'But don't be too rough. He's only a little People and he's probably hungry and frightened.' And he lowered David gently on to the grass.

At once the Shaggy Pups were all over him. They licked his face with great tongues like enormous pieces of wet sandpaper.

'Isn't he cute!' they wuffed, and 'Look at his funny little pink paws!'

By this time they had rolled David on to his back and one of the pups began to lick the soles of his bare feet while the other put out a big woolly paw and began to tickle his tummy. Now David is very, very ticklish, and this treatment almost sent him into hysterics.

'Ow, ow, ow!' he yelled, rolling about. 'Ow! Ooo! Stop it . . . stop it . . . Oh! Oh! Oh!'

'That will do, Pups,' barked a sharp voice. 'Leave the little thing alone now. It needs some rest. You can play with it later.'

'Can it sleep in our bed, Ma?' wuffed one of the Pups.

'In your bed? I should think *not* indeed,' snapped their mother. 'I don't want you covered in fleas!'

David was *furious*. 'Dogs don't get fleas from people,' he snapped. 'It's people who . . .'

But he got not further, for the mother dog had pushed a paw between his teeth and forced down his lower jaw. 'Why, they're only baby teeth!' she barked. 'I warn you, Shaggy Dog, I'm not going to wear my paws to the bone hunting special foods for a baby People. How do you think we're going to feed it?'

'There's no need to pamper it,' wuffed Shaggy Dog. 'It'll be quite happy to eat our left-overs – you'll see.'

'I can't see it cracking a bison's thigh-bone with those tiny teeth.'

'There are plenty of other things it *can* manage. Why, a little People like that could live for three days on half a rat . . .'

'And now,' barked Shaggy Dog, 'I'm going to have a nap and I'll take the People in the cave too, so it can get a snooze without you Pups disturbing it.'

'How long, Pop? How long? We want to play with it.' (That was the Pups.)

'Half an hour, Pups, to let it rest. Then you can play with your People as much as you want.' And Shaggy Dog picked up David and carried him off to the cave.

The last thing that he heard before Shaggy Dog dropped him gently down in a dark corner of the cave was a snatch of barkage between the Shaggy Pups:

'D'you think,' wuffed one of them, 'we could train the People to catch field-mice in its teeth and bring them back to us?'

'Of course,' answered the other. 'It'll be easy. Why, I'm sure *our* People understands every word we bark.'

Poor David! How he wished he *didn't*!

CHAPTER 7

TOBY TO THE RESCUE!

TOBY plodded through the forest. He was feeling cold without his dressing-gown. He was also feeling lonely, lost, more than a little scared, and hungry (but there was nothing unusual about *that*. Toby is hungry more often than any boy you can think of).

It was getting lighter now and the great forest seemed even more mysterious and frightening to him than it had done by moonlight.

Now and then he stopped and called as loudly as he could: '*Mr Strretch*! . . . Mis . . ter . . STRRE . . . E . . . E . . . E . . TCH!' And then he stood and waited and strained his ears for *ages*, but there was not even an echo.

Toby came at last to the crest of a small hill. Before him there was more and more forest with no trace of track. 'But I might be able to see further if I could get up higher,' he thought. So he chose the tallest of all the trees he could see and began to climb it. About half-way up he stopped to scan the way ahead. From here there *did* seem to be the faint line of a track: perhaps Mr Strretch was down there, perhaps not so far ahead after all.

Toby took a deep breath and shouted: 'Mr STRRE . . E . E . . ETCH! WHERE ARE YOOOOOOU?'

All that came in reply, however, was a furious squawking from some bird that his shouting had disturbed. High above him he could see the shape of a large and clumsily-made nest. He could see the bird's beak opening and shutting. He could see its wings fluttering angrily before it settled itself once more after being so rudely awakened.

No luck again! Toby began to climb down. And as he did so, there came again a great squawking from the bird above. There was a rending and snapping of twigs. A hole suddenly appeared in the bottom of the nest and from it there fell . . . an egg – an egg that made noises as it fell . . . an egg that fell past Toby crying in a small, but unmistakable voice: *'Help, me noble friend. Help! Save me from that feathered freak!'*

Toby slid down the tree at top speed, to find the 'egg' rolling around and bouncing madly up and down.

'Keep it off me, laddie,' cried Mr Strretch. 'I can't get back to me normal size until I get me breath back. That bird's been sitting on top of me all night. Look out! It's coming to get me!'

Toby snatched up a fallen branch – only just in time, for with cries of 'Ooooo-*kuk*! Ooo-*kuk*!' the bird came swooping down with eager claws outstretched. Toby drove it off, waving the branch menacingly while Mr Strretch rolled about panting, but gradually getting bigger and bigger.

'A thousand thanks, me brave companion,' gasped Mr Strretch. 'That foolish creature was determined to sit on me until I hatched out with a beak and wings. I was near to suffocation when I heard you call. It gave me renewed strength, Toby me boy. I managed to get out me cane and I jabbed at the bottom of that nest till I fell through. Ahhh . . . !' And with a great sigh of relief. Mr Strretch's hat and his head and his arms and his legs popped out and he was himself again.

'I was getting desperate too, Mr Strretch,' Toby admitted. 'I thought I'd never find you.'

'The feeling, me revered friend, was mutual,' declared Mr Strretch. 'As for that flying egg-collector . . . *why, just look at it*!'

Ever since Toby had driven it away, the Oookuk had been sitting on the branch of a nearby tree. As Mr Strretch grew and grew, the bird's eyes became wider and wide with surprise and joy. And now, as he spoke, it took off from its perch, flew on to his shoulder, and began to rub its head up and down against his cheek, burbling '*kuk-kuk-kuk-kuk-kuk*' in a very soppy manner.

'Hey, hey, hey!' cried Mr Strretch in great alarm. 'What's it doing this for, the frenzied feathered fathead? What's it all about . . . ?'

But Toby was helpless with laughter. Tears were running down his cheeks and he could scarcely find breath to reply.

'Oh, Mr St . . st . . st . . strretch!' he gasped. 'Can't you see? It th . . thinks it's hatched you. It l . . l . . loves you, Mr Strretch! You're its f . . f . . favourite, f . . f . . first-born ch . . ch . . *chick*!'

'WHAT!' roared Mr Strretch so loudly that the Oookuk shot straight up into the air. 'Have I not yet finished with this wandering warbler? Take wing, balmy bird! Fly! Hop it! Has it gone, me breathless friend?'

'It's flown away,' said Toby. 'Perhaps,' he added wickedly, 'it's gone to bring you some nice worms for your breakfast.'

Mr Strretch shuddered. 'Then let us speed away before it can return,' he begged. 'Call your brother – I take it he can't be far away – call him and let us go.'

That was an awful shock! For just those few minutes the thought of David's plight had gone completely out of Toby's head. He felt terribly guilty as he told Mr Strretch about the Great Beast and how, after David had helped him escape, he had seen the creature carrying his brother in the direction of Howling Valley.

'I must go to his rescue. At once!' said Toby desperately.

'Which way will you go, laddie?' asked Mr Strretch.

And Toby had to admit: 'I don't know.'

'But *I* do,' said Mr Strretch. 'I will guide you to Howling Valley. And when we get there we will spy out the land and make a plan to rescue our comrade David. Agreed? Then – quick march!' And he set off at a smart pace.

As Toby turned to march beside his friend he noticed something and he wondered if he should tell Mr Strretch what it was. He decided, however, that it was perhaps better not to say anything, since it might delay their search for David.

What Toby had noticed was this: the Oookuk had returned. It was at this moment sitting – with a fatuous smile on its beak – *on the top of Mr Strretch's stove-pipe hat.*

CHAPTER 8

THE MONSTER OF THE LAKE

To David it seemed no time at all before the Shaggy Pups were gambolling and wuffling around him, nosing him out into the grassy valley to play.

He was limp for lack of sleep but he knew he must try to keep alert so that he could seize any chance of escape that he saw. One thing he was *not* – he was not *hungry*: the idea of making a meal of half a cold, dead rat had put hunger right out of his head.

The longing for food didn't even come back to him when the Pups offered him a field-mouse they had caught. In Howling Valley a field-mouse was as large as a hare and when David saw how big its fangs were he hoped the Pups would forget all about their idea of setting him to chase such a creature.

'Come on, People,' wuffed one of the Pups jovially, 'get your teeth into it! Worry it, boy!'

'He seems afraid of it,' said the other. 'He's only a little People, you know. We'd better set him hunting something smaller.'

'Like bird-eating spiders, perhaps? Oh, well, we'll think about that later. Come on, People. We'll teach you some tricks.'

First they made David trot behind them. 'To heel, People!' they wuffed. Then when he'd mastered that, they would stop and say 'Die! People!' After they'd pushed him to the ground several times, David realised that 'Die!' meant that he had to flop on the ground, lie quite still and pretend to be dead. Then the Shaggy Pups would run about a hundred yards off and wuffle: 'Up, People! Come to heel!' and David was supposed to scramble to his feet and dash at top speed to join them.

When they got tired of this game – and David was

tired of it long before *they* were – the Pups had a brilliant idea.

They made him kneel and hold his head back. Then they balanced something on the end of his nose (David couldn't see what it was because the sun was in his eyes) and they wuffed 'Hup!' After a while David grasped the idea: he was supposed to jerk his head, sending the object into the air, and to catch it in his teeth as it fell.

Well, as you might expect, David was not at all clever at this, but the Pups were determined that he should learn and, as they were far too big for him to argue with, he just had to go on trying.

At last he managed it. With a jerk that made him feel his neck was breaking, David sent the thing high into the air and as it fell, his teeth closed firmly upon it with a *snap* and a *crrunch!* And with that *crrunch*, David realised what the object was: it was a very large snail-shell.

'Aaaah!' cried David, hurling the shell into the bushes. And he began rubbing his hands frantically across his mouth while the Shaggy Pups rolled over and over, yelping with laughter. David knelt there, fuming, until they had done and that pause enabled him to get his breath back a little. This was just as well, for one of the Shaggy Pups wuffed:

'Let's have a race. Over to the lake.'

'People can't run fast enough to make it a *real* race.'

'No, he can't. I wonder why he's so slow?'

'I reckon it's because a People only runs on two legs.'

'It should be able to run twice as fast on four, then!'

'Of course it should! Come on, People! Get your front paws down on the ground and we'll show you how to run properly!'

I'm very glad that you weren't there to see David, with his nose near the ground and his behind stuck up in the air, while the Shaggy Pups pranced around him or gave him encouraging shoves from the rear. It was most embarrassing.

At last they stopped by the side of the big lake and

David sat panting while the Shaggy Pups considered what to do next.

'People looks a bit hot,' wuffed one.

'A swim would do him good.'

'Could do with another swim myself.'

'Same here. Let People rest a while then we'll all go in.'

'All right.'

It seemed as if David was out of luck again. When the Pups first barked about his need for a swim, he had been weighing up his chances of escape by doing a fast crawl across the lake (David is quite a good swimmer). But from what the Pups said after that, it was clear that they could swim themselves. So he sat there, very fed up, while from the branches of a high tree across the lake some silly bird sat and chanted a monotonous call: . . . 'Oooo-*kuk!* . . . Ooo-*kuk!* . . . Ooo-*kuk!*' He looked at it angrily. It sounded so *pleased* with itself that he wanted to shout: 'Oh, shut up!'

The Pups called him:

'Come on, People!'

'Into the water!'

'Let's see how you can swim!'

They all plunged into the lake and David could see from the first moment that the Shaggy Pups were as much at home in the water as he was. They swam around him, doing the dog-paddle (as, of course, you'd expect) and when one of them dunked him, David dived under the Shaggy Pup and came up behind it. The Pups were delighted.

'People can swim, all right!' wuffed one.

'Yes. There's not much *else* he can do, but he *can* swim.'

David sat back and floated a moment, looking round the lake. He and the Shaggy Pups were the only creatures to be seen, except for that silly bird. Not far away there floated a half-submerged log. David decided he'd swim to it so he made off. The Pups didn't notice this move for a moment or so, then with joyful wuffs they came after him.

It was when David was within a couple of yards of the log that the dreadful thing happened.

The log seemed to glide suddenly towards him. The front part of the log rose into the air, and on its underside . . . now almost above David's head . . . he caught a panic-stricken glimpse of huge saw-like teeth. Horror gripped him!

The Shaggy Pups saw the movement of the vast jaws almost at the same time. They yelped together in terror . . .

'*Crocodile*!'

And, without a thought for David's plight they turned, thrashed their way to the shore and pelted, yelping, tails between their legs, towards the safety of the cave.

David jerked his head to one side as the great teeth came down with a steely *snap* and a splash. But he was not to escape.

Something below the water gripped his leg and he was drawn down . . . down beneath the cold waters of the lake!

CHAPTER 9

TERRIBLE NEWS!

THE grip around David's leg was like that of an iron hand. He was drawn down until he felt his lungs must burst. Then, just as suddenly, he was thrust upwards . . . upwards until he felt his head break water. He drew in a long, welcome breath and opened his eyes.

He was in complete darkness . . . and out of that darkness there came a sound. It was a sound he had feared he might never hear again.

It was the voice of Toby. 'Put your hand on my shoulder, David,' he said, 'and keep swimming.'

'Toby! Where are you? Where am I . . . ?'

'Where are you, me jolly snail-juggler?' came the voice of Archimedes Strretch from behind David. 'Why, you're nowhere else but inside the Toby-Strretch, Mark 1 Do-It-Yourself Crocodile! Keep those jaws moving, Toby me noble friend,' added Mr Strretch. 'And you, David, put a hand on Toby's shoulder and keep swimming, me laddie . . . keep pushing until we're out of sight of those overstuffed canine monstrosities and we can get into the shallows under the trees.'

As you can well imagine, David forgot all his tiredness and he struck out lustily, sending the Toby-Strretch, Mark 1 Do-It-Yourself Crocodile over the water at a spanking pace while Toby worked the great jaws, churning the water into white foam as it went along.

From their cave the Shaggy Pups crouched beside their father and mother, all shivering with fear as they peered out over the lake and watched the fearsome working of the crocodile's hungry jaws as it swam away.

'Poor People's been eaten!' wuffled one of the Pups.

'It you hadn't been looking at that silly little thing instead of keeping your eyes open for danger – as I'm for ever telling you to do,' snapped their mother, ' — you'd never have gone in the water at all.'

'I want another People,' snuffled one of the Pups.

'So do I. Catch us another People to play with, Pop.'

'You'll do no such thing!' barked their mother, as Shaggy Dog hesitated. 'What! Have another People trying to feed my Pups to a crocodile? I'd never have a moment's peace of mind!'

'Oh, go *on*, Pop.'

'You heard what your mother said.'

'Aw, Pop, *do*! Catch us another People, Pop! We want *another* People!'

Shaggy Dog stole a glance at the Pups' mother. Then he put his great head down close to theirs. He drew back his lips so that they could see his great big dripping fangs. And he growled:

'There's been nothing but trouble since I brought a People into this cave. Swimming right into a crocodile, indeed! If you can't train a People better than *that*, then you're not fit to have one. So stop pestering me and get out of my SIGHT!' And his growl as he said this last word was so loud that it rumbled the whole length of Howling Valley and set loose rocks tumbling down the cliffs.

And that was the end of *that*.

Smoothly and majestically the Toby-Strretch, Mark 1 Do-It-Yourself Crocodile sailed down towards the end of the lake where the forest closed around it.

There was a bend in the lake here and as the crocodile neared it there came a sudden great splash and, a moment later, piteous cries.

'Crocodile to the rescue!' cried Toby. 'Full speed ahead!'

The Mark 1 Do-It-Yourself Crocodile shot forward, sending out huge V-shaped ripples as it cleft the water.

'It's a little boy,' called Toby a moment later, as they rounded the bend. He peered ahead from his look-out position in the jaws of the crocodile. 'But . . . but . . . that's funny! He's got great white whiskers all over his face!'

'Save your breath, laddie,' panted Mr Strretch. 'Let's get this whiskered Whateveritis out of the water – *then* we can decide how old it is.'

David had managed a quick glimpse ahead over Toby's shoulder.

'It's gone under,' he said. 'Seeing the crocodile coming must have scared it to death. I'll dive for it while you get to the shore.'

And taking a deep breath, David ducked his head, kicked up his heels and struck out to the rescue. He soon spotted a rising spiral of air bubbles and followed them down to the lake bed. It was dark here and the water was murky but he could just distinguish a tiny leg and a tiny hand that gripped – of all odd things – a gleaming axe. The Whateveritis, as Mr Strretch had called it, was clearly unconscious. David grabbed an arm and, lungs bursting, made for the surface.

Already the Mark 1 Crocodile had been beached – and in the deep reeds at the water's edge it looked just as horrifying as it had done in the water. Mr Strretch and Toby waded out and helped David and his limp burden to the shore.

'Bless my boots and buttons!' declared Mr Strretch, as they rolled the creature on its back, 'this is surely the oldest small boy in creation!'

The creature was about two feet tall, and it was so broad that it looked almost as round as Mr Strretch's portly stomach. The face seemed to be all white whiskers and bushy white eyebrows while tight white curls peeped out from under a kind of leather nightcap. From the face right down to a pair of very stout, hobnailed boots, it was whiskers, whiskers, all the way.

'I'm afraid we reached him too late,' said Toby sadly, but David had dropped to his knees and was kneeling over the body.

'We must try the kiss of life,' he said. 'It may not be too late after all.'

It was difficult to find a mouth under all that whisker but David managed it and, opening the jaws, he bent his head and blew into the creature's lungs.

The result was vastly different from anything that the boys or Mr Strretch could have expected.

With a sudden terrific bound and a yell of fury the creature shot on to its feet, whirling the axe round its head so rapidly that it seemed to be in the centre of a gleaming circle of hissing steel. They saw then that this was no whiskered boy but a sturdy old gentleman – a sort of mini-man, so to speak, but a mini-man in a maxi-rage.

'Aaarrrr!' he yelled, 'would you seek the life of Elgrim, foul Spirits of the Water? Come in your thousands, this Elven blade shall cleave you to the chine!'

His furious prancing had taken him to the bank of the lake just above the reed-bed. And there his eyes suddenly fell on the Toby-Strretch, Mark 1 Do-It-Yourself Crocodile.

With a screech of '*Elgrim elohi elohiri*!!!!' the mini-

This is the sad fate of the Mark 1 Do-It-Yourself Crocodile, made by Toby and Mr Strretch. It looked so lifelike that Elgrim the Elf went for it with his axe. And, since it was only an imitation crocodile, it promptly sank and Elgrim was nearly drowned a second time. The moral of this story (for Elves, at any rate) is: Beware of Imitations!

man leaped on to its back and sank its shining axe-blade into its spine.

Now the Mark 1 Do-It-Yourself Crocodile was a very stout creature. Toby and Mr Strretch had built it with a framework of sturdy canes and its back and snout looked extremely life-like, with their covering of gnarled bark and grey lichen.

But when you attack a crocodile of this sort with a very sharp axe there is only one thing that can happen. It did – the Mark 1 Do-It-Yourself Crocodile promptly sank and, with a great gurgling cry, the mini-man went down with it.

He wasn't so long under the water this time, for Mr Strretch who had dashed to the water's edge when he saw the axe flashing down on to the back of the crocodile, grabbed him by the arm as he went under and hoisted him on to the bank.

The mini-man brushed his bushy eyebrows out of his eyes and looked up at Mr Strretch.

'Ho, Giant!' he panted, 'I thank thee for saving my life. Bear witness now that I, Elgrim the Elf, have slain the Monster of the Lake with mine own strong arm and mine axe Thuribor.'

'Not so fast, Elgrim!' said Mr Strretch. 'You should also thank me young friend here,' and he pointed to David. 'He's the one who dived in and saved you when the monster had dragged you to the bottom of the lake.'

Elgrim the Elf passed a hand across his eyes. 'Aye . . .I remember now,' he whispered. 'I went down and down, and all was dark and then I could not breathe . . .' He turned to David and raised an arm: 'I owe my life to you also, for Elves cannot swim. If I can do anything to help you – command me.'

'Oh, that's all right, Mr Elgrim,' said David, embarrassed. But Toby chimed in with a question.

'Could you tell us one thing, Mr Elgrim?' he asked, softly. '*If you can't swim, why did you go into such deep water*?'

Elgrim the Elf was clearly not prepared for such a question. He went very red in the face (such little bits of face as could be seen between his whiskers, that is) and he stood first on one foot and then on the other.

Finally he burst out: 'It shames me to tell! I was surprised while I slept and seized by two soldiers. They thought it a fine joke to fling me to my death in the lake and ride on.'

'I just can't imagine *anyone* doing an evil thing like that!' said David, shocked.

'These men would,' answered Elgrim the Elf. 'They would do that and much worse. Beware of them! They are camping in the forest at this very moment – *they and many others like them who carry the banners of Black Walter, the evil Baron of Bunkulm!*'

CHAPTER 10

THE TRICKERY OF ELGRIM THE ELF

'BLACK WALTER!' cried Toby.

'His troops . . . here in the forest!' said Mr Strretch, looking worried.

But David whooped: 'Hooray! Then we're on the track of the Golden Cactus already!'

'A Golden *Cactus*? A growing *plant* made of *gold*?' asked Elgrim the Elf. 'Come, can such a thing be possible?'

David was just about to reply that not all the cactus was gold, only the flowers, when Mr Strretch said loudly: 'Of course it isn't possible, me bold Elgrim! How could it be? The boy wasn't speaking of a golden *plant*! "The Golden Cactus" is the title of a very rare book . . .'

'But look here!' began David crossly, 'you said . . .' He didn't get any further because Toby kicked his ankle and whispered fiercely: 'Shut up!'

'Pray don't interrupt me, laddie,' said Mr Strretch severely. 'Yes, as I was saying, it's the title of a very rare book of myths and legends and the three of us have journeyed far to see it. We are told that this Baron has a copy, also that the Mayor of a village called Blumendorf possesses one . . . But if the Baron is an evil man, as you state . . .'

'You had far better go to Blumendorf,' said Elgrim. 'Keep away from that man at all costs. In any case he is not in the forest with these followers of his. They say he has gone off on some secret – and I doubt not, wicked – mission. Besides, the village you speak of is not far.'

'We had better hurry though, for the sun is sinking,' said Mr Strretch. 'Can you direct us there?'

'That I can!' replied Elgrim, very proudly. 'I will do better – I will mark the path for you.' He drew his axe from beneath his white beard. 'When daylight fades,' he said, 'the power of magic returns to the Elves. Go now, Thuribor, and mark a trail my friends can follow safely into Blumendorf.' And he flung the gleaming axe into the air.

Twice it circled round Elgrim's head, then it shot away among the trees.

'*Crack*!' went the axe against the trunk of one . . . then another . . . and another . . . And each time it sliced off a great sliver of bark so that a white patch showed.

As the boys and Mr Strretch watched in amazement they saw one white mark after another appear, blazing a clear trail through the forest as far as eye could see.

For a moment there was silence. And then, like a flash of light, Thuribor was circling once more over the head of Elgrim the Elf and nestling in his hand.

'Follow that trail,' said the Elf. 'You will be in Blumendorf before it is dark. Farewell – until we meet again.'

And before they could say a word in reply, Elgrim the Elf simply melted (as Toby said later 'like an ice-cream on a hot plate'), he melted into the ground and disappeared.

'Now quickly – on our way to Blumendorf and Captain Cobwebb's headquarters!' said Mr Strretch. 'And let's hope we don't fall into the hands of Black Walter's murderous soldiers on the way!'

But David had a bone to pick with Mr Strretch.

'Look here,' he said angrily, as they plodded along the trail, 'you know very well that the Golden Cactus *isn't* the title of a book! Why did you make it seem to Mr Elgrim that I was telling a lie? And why did you back him up, Toby, and kick me on the shin?'

'I'm sorry, me loyal laddie,' said Mr Strretch, '— but I had to do it and I'll tell you why. As soon as Elgrim showed an interest in the Golden Cactus I remembered something. I remembered that Elves live under the ground and they are famous workers in metals that are found in the earth – such as iron and silver and gold. But gold is rare, as you know, and the Elves will do anything to get their hands on it. They will lie and deceive and rob for it. They don't think it's wrong to do that kind of thing, because they believe that everything that comes from under the earth's surface belongs to them. They consider that creatures that live above ground have no right to it at all. That's why I told Elgrim there wasn't a Golden Cactus. If he thought there *was*, then he would be after it – and I reckon we've enough dangers to face in fighting Black Walter and his band without tackling an Elf as well.'

'I see,' said David. 'I'm sorry I mentioned the Golden Cactus in front of Elgrim. But I'm sure you put him off the scent.'

'I'm *not* sure you did,' said Toby, firmly. 'I've been suspicious of that whiskery old Elf for some time. That's why I kicked you, David, when you mentioned the Golden Cactus. To start with, Elgrim told us he was thrown into the water by Black Walter's soldiers.'

'Why should he lie about that, Toby me laddie?' asked Mr Strretch.

'Because he'd been spying on us,' said Toby. 'He wasn't chucked into the lake. He fell off the branch of a tree. *I saw him fall.* I'd felt for some time that someone was watching us, Mr Strretch,' said Toby, 'and I'm sure it was Elgrim. I think that when we were out of sight in the bushes, building the Mark 1 Crocodile, Elgrim got up the tree to keep watch. That's why I asked him how he came to be in the water. He couldn't very well tell the truth so he made up that story about soldiers throwing him in.'

'Are you really sure about this?' said David. 'I mean, *really* sure that you saw him fall from the tree?'

'Of course I'm sure,' snapped Toby. 'And there's another thing – he said the soldiers threw him into the water and then rode away. Well, I looked in the soft mud at the edge of the lake and there were no marks of horses' hooves, in fact, no signs of a struggle at all.'

'A noble piece of detective work!' declared Mr Strretch. And David said: 'Hear, hear!' He thought his brother was very smart indeed.

'So I think Elgrim is a very suspicious character,' said Toby. 'And,' he added, 'it makes me wonder about this trail that he blazed for us . . .'

'What about it?' said Mr Strretch, quickly.

'Well,' said Toby. 'I wonder . . . I wonder, does it *really* go to Blumendorf, like he said? Suppose Elgrim wanted to get us lost in the forest . . . to have us out of his way while he found out the truth about the Golden Cactus? Suppose . . .'

He got no further. David with a sudden shout, had seized his shoulder and was pointing here, there, everywhere around . . . 'Look . . . ! *Look* . . . ! LOOK!'

So far, there had been a clear trail of white-marked trees. But now every tree in the forest . . . every one they could see – in front of them, on either side, behind them . . . wherever they looked – *every single tree bore the scar of Thuribor, the magic axe of Elgrim*!

The wily Elf had led them into a trap. The marked path had vanished. They were utterly lost.

CHAPTER 11

ORDEAL BY FIRE!

'*Now* what do we do, me laddies?' asked Mr Strretch.

'Let's try this direction,' suggested David.

'No – let's go this way,' said Toby.

'Then I say let's go *no* way,' decided Mr Strretch, '— at least not until we've all had a rest. Come on – sit down. You can tell us what happened to you, David, among those great beasts in Howling Valley.'

So David told his story and Mr Strretch told of his capture by the Oookuk and Toby told how he found Mr Strretch and they both went in search of David.

'We built the Mark 1 Crocodile,' said Toby, 'because we'd seen the Shaggy Pups swimming earlier and when they started playing with you we felt sure they'd bring you over to the lake. Weren't they scared!'

'So was I!' said David, '— and so was Elgrim!'

The name of Elgrim chilled their hearts with fear and they were silent. At last Toby said, slowly: 'You know, as long as we stop here we're doing what Elgrim wants us to do. I'm sure he just expects us to stay put, thinking we're lost and afraid of moving . . .'

'All right, then, me wise young warrior,' put in Mr Strretch. 'Let's go – but which way shall we go?'

'Why, *any* way!' said David. 'If he's trying to keep us here, then which ever way we go he'll try to stop us. We'll soon find out if Toby's right. Which way, Toby? You choose!'

'Then follow me!' cried Toby, and in the fading light of evening, he plunged ahead among the trees.

Hardly had he moved than a great crashing broke out in the undergrowth ahead. There was a burst of terrifying sound, a fearful mixture of snarl and hiss and roar . . .

And suddenly, right in front of them, there loomed the most frightening creature they had ever seen. It was like a giant lizard. The scaly body, green and luminous, stretched back into the shadows where a heavy tail thrashed among the bushes. And from that body there rose – much taller than Toby – a long, snake-like neck covered in glowing yellow spots. Two curious wings vibrated on each side of a great horned head and from the beast's vicious snout there shot a jet of flame and smoke.

Toby stood rooted to the spot in horror, choking in a blast of heat. David shouted: 'I'm coming, Toby!' and leaped to seize his brother's arm and pull him out of the way.

But Mr Strretch was quicker. 'Back! Both of you!' he shouted. He leaped between them and thrust both boys behind him. 'Get stones for ammunition!' he cried, and with slashing cane he faced the monster.

But from the start it was a hopeless battle. Although David and Toby rained the heaviest stones they could find upon the beast, it did not halt. Although Mr Strretch lunged and struck again and again, the flying head of the Fire-Lizard dodged every blow. Mr Strretch and the boys were forced back and back.

Suddenly, David got an idea – a desperate idea.

'Your hat, Mr Strretch!' he shouted. 'Use your hat!'

'Me hat? Me hat?' Mr Strretch was puzzled. Then it came to him. 'Ah, yes!' he panted. 'It's the last hope, but . . . *here* goes!'

And, ducking swiftly to one side, Mr Strretch managed to grip one of the wings on the Fire-Lizard's head, while with the other hand he whipped off his tall stove-pipe hat and rammed it down over the beast's snout and eyes.

For a moment the gloom of the forest was broken only by the green and yellow glow from the Fire-Lizard's hide. For a moment the snarling and hissing was so muffled that the forest seemed almost quiet again.

Then, with a *sssssshhh! – sssshhHHH! –* and a great jet of flame, the Fire-Lizard blew Mr Strretch's smouldering hat high into the air. And at that moment, high above their heads, they heard a sudden shriek.

'Ooooooo! Ooooooo!' came a bird-like screech of fury. 'Ooooooo! Ooooooo-KUK! KUK-KUK-KUK!!!'

And as the hat went up, down in a power-dive screamed the Oookuk and drove its steely beak into the Fire-Lizard's skull! With a despairing hiss and a choking snarl, the beast that Elgrim's magic had created fell limp and lifeless to the ground.

Mr Strretch picked up his battered hat with a deep sigh of relief. It was smouldering around the crown, but he stubbed out the glowing sparks in the damp grass and set it firmly on his head while the Oookuk fluttered anxiously around.

'Ooo-kuk!' it burbled caressingly, 'Ooo-ooo-ooo-ooo-*ooo*-kuk!' And it nestled on his shoulder and rubbed its head against his cheek.

'You see, David,' giggled Toby, 'I was right – the Oookuk thinks it hatched Mr Strretch out of an egg. It's very proud of him because he's grown into such a big chick . . .'

'Oh, spare me blushes, me teasing young friend!' protested Mr Strretch. His nose glimmered, deeply red, through the gloom.

'It must be true,' said David. 'Look how it flew to defend you and kill the Fire-Lizard.'

'What would have happened if it *hadn't* . . . ? asked Toby.

'Say no more! I tremble to think of it,' declared Mr Strretch. 'Why, that crawling volcano would have burned me to a cinder.' He stroked the Oookuk's plumage. 'Many thanks, me feathered fighter!' he said. 'From now on I consider meself adopted. And if you want to roost on the top of me hat . . . well, it's all yours, rent-free.'

But the Oookuk seemed worried. It flew up in the air and hovered as if it were listening. Then it flew back a little way along their trail and returned to them, *kuk-kuk-king* with annoyance.

'You'd think it was expecting someone!' said Toby.

It was fortunate that the Oookuk was there to slay the Fire Dragon for as you can see, Mr Strretch's hat failed to stifle the jet of flame when he jammed it over the beast's snout. Be warned by this! It is a waste of money to buy a hat for a hot-headed person.

'Yes, and it was annoyed because they were late,' added David.

The Oookuk fluttered down on to Mr Strretch's shoulder and clucked sharply: 'Ooo . . . kuk-KUK.' Then rising high among the trees, it vanished swiftly back along the way they had come.

'Now *what* do you make of *that*?' asked Mr Strretch.

But David was imitating the bird, 'Ooo . . . kuk-KUK,' he went. 'Why – it sounds as if it were saying: "You stay here." '

'That's what we'd better do, in any case,' suggested Toby. If Elgrim is going to produce a Fire-Lizard every time we start to march we *need* the Oookuk around!'

'Then let us lean back against this tree and try to get a little snooze,' said Mr Strretch. He looked at David and Toby. 'I don't know *what* me revered friend Captain Cobwebb is going to say when he sees us . . . Toby in pyjamas and wellington boots, David ditto but barefoot! Don't your feet hurt, David, me laddie?'

'A bit,' said David, sturdily. 'But I'll manage.' (They were very sore indeed, but he wasn't going to say so.)

'And as for me,' said Mr Strretch. 'I'm as charred as burnt toast and as smoked as a kipper. Oh, for a change of clothing . . . a wash . . a table spread with delicate dishes . . .!'

'Rrrrrrrrrrrr . . Hrrmph!' That was David snoring.

'Rrrrrr . . roast-beef . . . rrrr . . Yorkshire pudding . . . rrrrr . . . *yum-yum*.' *That* was Toby snoring *and* talking in his sleep.

Mr Strretch looked at them for a moment, then he lay back against the tree-trunk, pulled his stove-pipe hat down over his eyes and he said (you've guessed it) . . . 'Rrrrrrrr'.

And far down the trail behind them flew the Oookuk, sleepless, eagerly calling . . . tirelessly searching for *something*. But *what*?

CHAPTER 12

IN THE HANDS OF THE BLACK WARRIORS

THEY woke with a start – all three of them and all at once. And what woke them was not the chill of dawn or the first pale beams of sunlight against their eyes. It was the sharp tip of a sword-blade upon their chests.

'Death for the first who moves!' growled a deep voice.

Behind the sword-blades stood three frightening figures in black – black peaked helmets, close-fitting jerkins and hose of fine black chain-mail. All about them, save for the gleaming sword-blades, was black: even their faces had been painted in weird stripes and patterns of black to make them look more terrible. There could be no doubt who they were. The boys knew it even before the leader spoke:

'What do ye in the domains of Black Walter, Baron of Bunkulm?' he grated.

'A thousand apologies, me noble warriors,' answered Mr Strretch. 'We never meant to trespass on any man's land. We're three poor travellers, lost in the forest. And if you could put us on the road to Blumendorf we'd be most grateful, worthy Captain.'

'Ah!' said the leader. 'To Blumendorf . . . no doubt to look at a book of legends about a Golden Cactus . . . ?'

'Why, that's exactly it, Captain . . .'

'Silence!' roared the soldier. 'No doubt of it – these are the ones that he spoke of. Rope them firmly!'

One of the soldiers sprang forward, slipping a large coil of rope from his shoulder and began to lash Mr Strretch and the two boys tightly to the tree.

For a moment there was silence. Then Toby said, in a loud, complaining voice: 'Hey you! What's wrong with wanting to look at a silly old book, anyway? You just tell me what's so wrong about it?'

It was an dangerous trick – but it worked.

The captain raised his sword, quivering with anger.

'Right well you know it is no book you seek!' he roared. 'It is the Golden Cactus itself. Even a whiskered old Elf could see through *that* story.'

'There you see!' Toby whispered to David. '. . . Elgrim is behind this.'

David was so angry he forgot to keep his voice down: 'I'd like to get my hands on that Elgrim!' he snorted.

There was a burst of evil laughter from the soldiers.

'You will have a chance to meet him very soon, my young cockerel!' said the Captain. 'We made the Elf swear loyalty to Black Walter, to guard him and his treasure, the Golden Cactus, against such thieves as you. When we leave we will send Elgrim to you – he can prove his loyalty by slitting your throats.'

He turned to his companions. 'Come, lads,' he said, 'with the Elf to guard our rear we can join our comrades on the way to the Castle.'

And without another glance at the helpless captives, Black Walter's warriors strode off through the forest.

Mr Strretch and the boys listened anxiously until their footsteps had died away. Then Mr Strretch said cheerfully, 'Ah, well. Now that they're out of the way, we'd better get moving.'

'Moving!' said David. 'I can't stir a muscle.'

'They've tied us up so tight that my arms and legs are all pins and needles,' grumbled Toby.

'Don't worry, me laddies,' said Mr Strretch. 'I'll have you untied in a minute. I shall shrink . . . and shrink . . . and shrink,' he said, and he drew in his hat and head and arms and legs and first he became a large ball, and then he began to get smaller and smaller until the ropes simply collapsed on the ground and he rolled out from among them.

'And there we are!' chirruped Mr Strretch, rolling round and round and growing bigger and bigger again. 'Nobody ever tied up The Indiarubber Man for very long! I'll have those ropes off you in no time.'

When he had freed them, David and Toby stood rubbing their limbs to get the blood flowing again while Mr Strretch stood peering among the trees trying to decide which direction to take.

Suddenly Toby said: 'Listen!'

So far away that they could hardly hear it, there was a sound that was hauntingly familiar. It came again, closer . . . and again . . .

'It's the Oookuk, Mr Strretch!' cried David.

'Why, so it is,' said Mr Strretch, delightedly. 'And blesss my boots and buttons – listen to *that*! I do declare the blessed bird is bringing a visitor!'

As the Oookuk came nearer they could hear the sound of someone – or something – following it. Whatever it was, it made a good deal of noise.

The Oookuk suddenly came in sight, winging swiftly towards them. It circled over them twice, then fluttered down on to the top of Mr Strretch's hat, where it sat *kuk-kuk-kuk*-ing in triumph.

And behind it, blundering clumsily through the trees, several feet above the ground, there came . . .

'The Flying Basket!' David was jumping with delight.

'But however did the Oookuk manage to get it to *come* here?' Toby asked in amazement. 'I mean, surely they couldn't talk together?'

'Why not, me noble friend?' asked Mr Strretch. 'Why should you doubt this simple fact? You know what *I* say and I know what *you* say. That's because we're the same kind of creature. Right? So why shouldn't the Oookuk and the basket understand each other? They're the same kind of creature, aren't they? They've both got wings, haven't they? They both *fly*, don't they?'

Toby could only say weakly: 'Yes – I suppose so,' for this whirlwind of questions had left his head spinning.

The Flying Basket hovered over them for a moment, then it folded its great wings and sank slowly to the ground.

'In you get!' said Mr Strretch. 'The Flying Basket knows the way to Captain Cobwebb. Our troubles are over. Off you go and I'll follow behind.'

'What do you mean?' said David. 'We're not going unless you come with us.'

'But, me loyal friend,' said Mr Strretch. 'As you know, the Flying Basket can't carry three of us – remember how we tumbled down into this forest! It can lift the two of you, that's all.'

'But we *can't* leave you to have your throat cut by that awful Elf,' Toby protested.

'Hum! That *would* be most unpleasant,' said Mr Strretch. 'I know . . . take a length of this rope that we were tied up with. You get in the basket and fasten one end. I will walk on the ground holding the other. Then the Flying Basket can carry *you* and guide *me* . . . and I hope we shall all be back with Captain Cobwebb before nightfall.'

This seemed a very sound idea, so the boys climbed into the basket and very soon the great wings were carrying them slowly, but safely, many feet above the ground. David had tied one end of the long rope to the rim of the basket. Down below Mr Strretch had tied the other end around his wrist and he stepped forward confidently on the trek to safety.

After a time the Flying Basket emerged from the forest over fields. The sun came out and warmed them all.

In the basket David and Toby curled up on the seat and snoozed. Below them Mr Strretch stumbled along the ground in a doze. Even the Oookuk, sitting watchful in the top of his hat, at last put its head under its wing and fell asleep.

And that is why none of them had any warning at all when the Flying Basket soared serenely out over the edge of a deep canyon, with a rushing river far below.

Mr Strretch, the rope fastened to his wrist, walked blindly into space – and down he went with a yell of terror. That, and the squawk of the Oookuk as it shot panic-stricken into the air, woke David and Toby as the Flying Basket felt the sudden added weight of Mr Strretch. It lurched, tried to keep height, but couldn't and . . . down they all hurtled into the green water.

They came to the surface battling for breath. David

and Toby managed to grab the rim of the basket. Half submerged, it raced madly along through the surging rapids, dragging the helpless Mr Strretch behind at the end of the rope, while the Oookuk wheeled above them with piteous cries.

David gasped: 'Hang on, Toby!'

'I'm . . . trying . . .' said Toby weakly.

And then it seemed as if the end had really come. From above the water something huge and heavy fell upon them, cramming them all together and pulling them down.

They were trapped in the folds of a huge net . . . a net that was pulling them, tumbling them, over boulders . . . into the shallows . . . into the sunlight. Then suddenly, the three adventurers were tipped out like fish on to warm, dry sand.

And, as if in a dream, the boys heard a deep voice say calmly, and in a very superior manner:

'Pray have the goodness to inform Captain Cobwebb that his nephews have arrived.'

CHAPTER 13

NEW SUITS FOR NEW PERILS

ALTHOUGH David and Toby were bruised, breathless, wet and weary, the sound of Captain Cobwebb's name brought them to their feet.

Facing them was the man who had spoken. He was tall and thin, with flowing white hair and he was dressed in a tight suit of crimson velvet with a very large collar, scalloped and edged with gold, and bearing the golden initials 'C.C.'. Some way behind him a huge, black-haired man dressed in a leopard-skin was folding up the net in which he had dragged them to land. A wide green lawn swept up from the beach to a long, low thatched house built of great blocks of rough-hewn stone and set among trees.

Mr Strretch stepped forward between them and the man in red.

'Having removed this unwelcome trout from me weskit pocket,' he remarked, flipping the fish into the river, 'permit me, Mr Mysto, to introduce me dauntless companions: Mr David Green and Mr Toby Green. Boys, this is the One and Only Mr Mysto, Steward to the House of Cobwebb.'

'Hello, Mr Mysto,' said David and Toby together. 'Are you going to take us to Uncle Septimus now?'

'Welcome,' said Mr Mysto. 'You will meet Captain Cobwebb, your uncle, a little later when we dine. But first you need a bath and some new clothes. In the meantime, one wet dressing-gown between two boys will not do at all. Permit me,' he said, taking off David's dripping dressing-gown. 'A little stroking – thus – and *thus* – and a gentle shake – *so* – and we have *two* dressing-gowns. Silk, of course, as befits the House of Cobwebb.'

'I wish *I* could do that,' said David, as he put on the new dressing-gown.

'Oh, that's nothing to Mysto the Mystifying,' declared Mr Strretch. 'D'you know, me boy, he once pulled a string of sausages *and* the flags of all nations from me left ear. No wonder I'd been a little deaf on that side!'

'Thanks, Mr Mysto,' said Toby – but really he had something more important on his mind than dressing-gowns conjured from the air.

'I say, Mr Mysto,' he asked, 'will it be a long time before we eat?'

'Before we *dine*,' answered Mr Mysto, rather reprovingly. 'Yes, it will be a little time. But why not have a snack while you are waiting? I understand that you like to keep sausage-rolls in your wellingtons. Have you ever tried storing hot-dogs there? It improves the flavour tremendously.'

'They wouldn't stay hot, though,' Toby objected.

'Then stop a moment and let us see,' said Mr Mysto. And stooping down he pulled, from the top of Toby's wellingtons, two steaming hot-dogs. 'Pray try these,' he added, handing one to Toby and one to David. 'I trust the mustard will be to your liking.'

'It's super!' Toby said as he took a big mouthful. And a moment later he sighed: 'Never mind dressing-gowns – I wish I could do things like *this*!'

Mr Mysto beamed with pleasure at this compliment. He paused to speak to the man in the leopard-skin as they passed him.

'We shall need more logs for the great fireplace, Mr Muscle,' he said. 'Will you kindly see to it?'

'Sure,' said the other cheerfully. 'It's-a simple.' He nodded with a smile to David and Toby. 'You just-a watch,' he said, and he strode across to the foot of a dead, gnarled old oak. He stooped, curled one arm around the trunk and then, with a sudden jerk, wrenched the whole tree from the ground and set off towards the house.

'That's a little too long, I fear, Mr Muscle,' warned Mr Mysto.

'Then I make-a him in little-a pieces, Like-a-*so*!' answered Mr Muscle. And he broke the tree-trunk into three sections across his knee as if it had been a match-stick.

In the house they left Mr Strretch to go to his own quarters while Mr Mysto led them up a wide oak stair-case to a large bedroom with a quaint dormer window that peeped out from under the thatched roof.

'Through here is the bathroom,' said Mr Mysto. 'Fresh clothing will be waiting for you when you come out. And now, excuse me. I must speak to the cooks about this evening's banquet in your honour.'

'Cooks!' sighed Toby, as they wallowed in the hot, soapy water. 'Not just *a* cook, David . . . he said *cooks*, as if there were dozens of them!'

'And he didn't just say "dinner" – did you notice *that*?' David said. 'He said *banquet*. That's a kind of super-dinner, isn't it?'

'Yes. Lord Mayors have banquets,' said Toby (he knows quite a bit about matters connected with eat-ing), 'and Prime Ministers go to them sometimes – when they're invited. I wish *I* was a Lord Mayor. I wish I was Lord Mayor of London – he has the biggest banquets of anybody.'

'But they always have turtle soup at *his* banquets,' David reminded his brother, 'and you don't like it. We once had a tin of it and you said it tasted horrible.'

'I wouldn't *have* to have it if I was Lord Mayor. It'd be *my* banquet, so I'd be boss. I'd just order two helpings of something else I liked better, instead. Perhaps three . . .'

As they were drying themselves, a flick of David's towel knocked his dressing-gown from a chair and something bounced heavily from the pocket on to the floor.

'What are those? Stones?' asked Toby, as David picked them up.

'A couple of souvenirs from Howling Valley,' said David. 'I thought they'd gone forever when Mr Mysto turned my old dressing-gown into these two new ones. Here . . . catch!'

'Thanks,' said Toby, turning the stone over in his hand, 'But what made you pick these up?'

'Well, they're rather special ones,' said David. 'I call them Dog Stones. You see, the Shaggy Dogs and the Pups too, were always hunting this particular kind of stone. When they found one they'd lick away at it for half an hour at a time.'

'Why?' asked Toby, looking at his stone with disgust.

'I don't know. It's very rough. Perhaps they just like rubbing their tongues on it. Or it may have some kind of taste – salty, perhaps. Why not lick it and see?'

'Try it yourself! I don't want to taste Shaggy Dogs' tongues! Uh!' said Toby.

'Neither do I,' said David. 'Come on, let's get ready for the banquet.'

In the bedroom they found two complete suits of clothes awaiting them – and what clothes!

The shirts were of silk (with their initials worked on them in golden thread). The suits were of supple green suede leather – a jerkin that fitted closely round the neck, and tight-fitting trousers of the same material. There were soft suede shoes, whose tops stuck out in a kind of 'V' well above the ankle. And for each boy there was a broad belt with a golden buckle, and a jaunty leather cap with a peaked crown and a long goose-feather stuck in one side. In the front of each cap were the letters 'C.C.' in gold.

No two boys ever got dressed more quickly, and David and Toby were marching up and down, admiring each other, when Mr Strretch came in, pink and glowing. His high stove-pipe hat had been brushed until it was brilliantly black and shiny. His new check suit dazzled the eyes and his red velvet waistcoat – charred and ruined by the burning breath of the Fire-Lizard – had been replaced by an even more magnificent one of brilliant blue.

'Mr Strretch, you look wonderful!' cried Toby.

'Marvellous!' said David. 'How do you like *our* new outfits?'

Mr Strretch stuck his monocle in his left eye and walked round and round them.

'Superb . . . most excellent . . . Savile Row could not do better,' he said. 'And let me add – in those costumes you will be able to flit through the forest like shadows. *As you will need to do, me noble friends,*' he added. '*As you will need to do in the friendless days that lie ahead*!'

Mr Strretch dropped his voice very low when he said these last words and they both felt a chill run down their spines.

Before they could question him, Mr Strretch went on: 'Captain Cobwebb – your Uncle Septimus – has sent me to bring you to the banquet. There you will learn, me brave companions, of the fearful task that next awaits you! *Come . . .*'

CHAPTER 14

SECRET ORDERS

WHEN they came to the head of the staircase that led down into the great hall, the boys gasped. At the end of the hall, a huge log fire blazed in a vast fireplace. Torches flared from sconces on the walls on each side of the room. And right down the centre was a long, long oaken table with rows of high-backed chairs at each side and at the head one special chair, taller than all the rest with the initials C.C. engraved in gold on the back.

Behind every chair there stood a man. A strange assortment of people they were! David and Toby recognised Mr Mysto, of course, as he stood behind the chair marked C.C. There was the huge man, Mr Muscle, in his leopard-skin . . . another, in a gleaming silver shirt, who was amusing himself juggling with two plates, a knife and fork and a couple of wine-glasses . . . There was a tall, thin, wiry man with a brown face under a large Stetson hat, who carried a great coil of rope around one shoulder . . . another man with a turban, but bare to the waist and wearing long baggy trousers. His chest glowed red ('as if he was all lit up inside' whispered Toby). Another wore a great clown's hat . . . and another had round his shoulders loops of iron chain festooned with padlocks of all sizes.

As the boys went down the stairs they saw Mr Mysto suddenly pull back the chair at the head of the table as if to let somebody pass him. And then, from in front of the chair, there came a voice . . . a deep voice, a voice that seemed to be chuckling with every word it spoke.

'Welcome, David and Toby. Welcome to the House of Cobwebb. Welcome from your Uncle Septimus Cobwebb and all his friends assembled!'

'Welcome . . . welcome . . .!' cried all the people around the great table.

'Be seated all,' said the voice of Captain Cobwebb, as Mr Mysto pushed the big chair forward. 'David, Toby, come and sit at either side of me. Come near, too, Mr Strretch: we shall have something important to ask you. But that comes later. First, let us see that these hungry young adventurers dine well. Call the cooks, Mr Mysto, please!'

Mr Mysto raised a hand, and into the great hall there began to troop a seemingly endless file of men in white aprons and tall white hats, each bearing a large silver salver on which was his own special offering. Through another door came liveried footmen to stand behind each chair and serve the diners. It was a magnificent scene.

The only time that either boy spoke during that banquet was when David said:

'Uncle Septimus, *why* can't we see you?' And Toby chimed in: 'And why don't *you* eat anything? Why does Mr Mysto keep putting empty plates in front of you and then taking them away?'

There was a laugh at this that ran all round the table. Captain Cobwebb chuckled (and I can tell you it's quite an eerie thing to hear a chuckle coming out of the air).

'Well, boys,' he said. 'I suppose I've lived so long among invisible folk that I've just become that way myself. As to the food, what else would invisible people eat except invisible food? Those plates weren't empty to me!'

Finally, when the meal was over – and Toby was beginning to wish he could be hungry all over again so that he could start eating all over again – Mr Mysto called:

'Silence for Captain Cobwebb!'

'And now,' said Captain Cobwebb, 'I call on our good friend and comrade, Mr Strretch, for his report. Have the boys passed the test of courage, Mr Strretch? Are they fit to pass on to the next and more dangerous stage of this adventure?'

Mr Strretch stood up, fixed his monocle firmly in his

eye and leaned forward, his hands spread wide on the table.

'Indubitably, Captain,' he said weightily. 'Indubitably and of a definite certainty, without the barest hint of a shadow of a doubt and defying contradiction with all the power at my command, I say, Captain, that they have passed the test of courage. And I can't say fairer than *that*!' ended Mr Strretch, to a round of cheers from the guests.

'Then, David and Toby,' said Captain Cobwebb, 'you will depart tomorrow on the next stage of your adventure. It will be much more dangerous than the first. Let me tell you why.'

'We have news that the evil Baron Walter is on his way to his stronghold, Castle Doom. It stands on a rocky island in the middle of Boiling Lake, high in the mountains to the north of the Baron's territory of Bunkulm. The Baron is followed by a strong rearguard of his black warriors. But also on the way to the Castle Doom, by devious pathways of his own, goes Elgrim the Elf, lured by greed of gold.

'It is your task to wrest the Golden Cactus from the Black Baron, to keep it out of the hands of Elgrim and to bring it safely back to the people of Blumendorf. What is more, you must carry out the most perilous part of this mission *alone*, without any help from me. Are you prepared?'

'We're ready, Uncle Septimus!' said David.

'Rely on us!' said Toby. (After such a banquet he was ready to face wild tigers single-handed.)

'Then it is agreed,' said Captain Cobwebb. 'Clear the hall, my friends, and let us entertain our young adventurers.'

At once the other diners began to move away the chairs and the great table. Captain Cobwebb's chair was moved to the far end of the hall where the boys joined him.

'Do you like circuses?' asked Captain Cobwebb.

'Oh yes!' said Toby.

'And fairgrounds, too,' David added.

'And so do I,' said their Uncle Septimus heartily, '– always have done. When I was a boy I'd walk miles and miles to see a circus. But I fear that fairgrounds and circuses are going out of fashion. Every year more and more of them have to close down. And when they *do*, my boys, what happens to all those clever people who used to give us such pleasure? Why, they come here to the House of Cobwebb! Music, please, Mr Mysto!'

And with a blare of martial music there began the most wonderful show that David and Toby had ever seen. The juggler did incredible things. The man in the Stetson hat spun his rope in huge loops and jumped in and out of them. The man in the turban blew great flames from his mouth. The man with the chains allowed David and Toby to fasten him up and padlock his chains in a dozen different ways and each time he escaped from his bonds. The One and Only Mr Mysto put Mr Muscle in a box and sawed right through it – and Mr Muscle stepped out unhurt and picked up Mr Mysto on the palm of one hand. It was a terrific show.

Finally the performance ended and Captain Cobwebb bade goodnight to his guests.

'But stay with me and Mr Strretch, boys,' he said, 'I have something more to say to you.'

When the room had emptied, they sat before the dying fire and Captain Cobwebb said: 'Remember, both the troops of Black Walter and that wily Elf, Elgrim, will be on the look-out for you. In order to confuse them and make their task more difficult, you must each travel by a different route. Your paths link up at a ruined tower near Boiling Lake. From there you will make the final assault on Castle Doom together. You will each find a map in your tunic: memorise your route and destroy the map. Was there anything else, Mr Strretch?'

'Weapons, Captain,' said Mr Strretch.

'Ah, yes. Your best weapons will be your wits and your courage, of course,' said Captain Cobwebb. 'Apart from these you may have only those things that a boy would normally have in his pockets. What did we decide about that, Mr Strretch?'

‘One pocket-knife,’ said Mr Strretch, promptly. ‘One piece of string; a stone or pebble . . .’

‘We’ve each got a stone,’ said David.

‘Cross that out, then,’ said Mr Strretch. ‘What next? Oh, yes – a piece of chewing-gun, screwed up in silver paper, and a glass marble. That’s all.’

‘They are duly placed in the boys’ pockets,’ said Captain Cobwebb – and they were, too, for David and Toby at once plunged their hands in to find out.

‘What now?’ said Captain Cobwebb suddenly.

The boys looked up. Mr Mysto was standing beside them.

‘Elgrim the Elf is moving more swiftly than we had expected,’ he said. ‘There is no time for sleep. The boys must move tonight – and quickly.’

So it was that David and Toby found themselves trekking through the night towards the distant moonlit hills. And to face the might of Black Walter’s army and the wiliness of Elgrim the Elf each boy had only five weapons: a pocket-knife, a piece of string, a lump of chewing-gum, a stone and a glass marble. What possible use could *they* be?

CHAPTER 15

A TRAP IN THE TREE-TOPS

AT length the two boys reached the spot where the track divided. Toby’s way lay to the left, down towards the river which he would have to cross. David’s path went upwards through wooded slopes towards the hills.

‘Well, this is it,’ said David. ‘This is where we part. But I don’t like it.’

‘Neither do I,’ said Toby.

‘But we said we’d go through with it . . .’

‘Yes. So . . .’

‘Here goes, then,’ said David. ‘First man to reach the

ruined tower waits two days for the other one. If the other hasn't arrived, then he makes the attempt on Castle Doom on his own.'

'Right.'

So they shook hands – like all comrades do when they part, each to face danger and death alone – and they set off without a backward look.

As Toby made his way to the river he was thinking furiously. From what Mr Mysto had said, it seemed that Elgrim was getting near. Toby was tired and needed sleep and in the gloom of the woodlands he could not travel fast. Elves usually move by night and after sunset they have their magic to help them, too. So if Toby kept going during the night, Elgrim might well steal up on him from behind and he would be at the mercy of the Elf and his magic axe, Thuribor.

'But if I sleep now,' he told himself, 'I shall be fresh when daylight comes and Elgrim will probably have to stop to get some sleep. Then I may be able to sneak past him, or . . . or . . . *I'll deal with him*!' Toby wasn't sure how he would deal with Elgrim but when he thought of the Elf's treachery, his blood boiled.

He plodded along the river bank until he came to a spot where there was a small island in mid-stream. 'This will do,' he told himself. 'It's close enough to the other bank for me to keep an eye on the track and Elgrim can't attack me here because Elves can't swim. He told David so himself.'

So Toby settled down in a patch of long grass and slept with an easy mind.

He was awakened suddenly, shortly before dawn, by the sound of a voice. Toby peeped out. Whoever was coming along the woodland was too far away for the words to be heard distinctly, but Toby had no doubt whose voice it was! It was Elgrim, chanting a dreary, monotonous marching song as he plodded in the wake of Black Walter's troops. Nearer and nearer he came and now Toby could hear the words:

'Gold! Gold!
We seize it for ourselves!
For gold is not for human-kind —
It's only for us Elves!'

'You just wait, Elgrim,' muttered Toby. '*I'll* show you whose gold it is! The Golden Cactus is going back to the poor people of Blumendorf!'

He crouched lower in the grass. The Elf had stopped almost opposite Toby's hiding place and was wrestling with some branches that barred his path. Evidently the way was too overgrown for him to get through, for after a few moments of grumbling he stepped back and Toby saw the flash of Elgrim's magic axe. Raising it above his head the Elf cried:

'Go clear a track, O Thuribor,
That I may safely tread.
And should another trespass there —
Slice off his saucy head!'

The axe flew from his hand – and Toby could hear the *swish . . . swish* of its blade as it sliced a clear pathway through the bushes and undergrowth while Elgrim marched forward again with his threatening chant of '*Gold! Gold!*'

Toby chuckled. And then he began to sing softly:

'You cleared a track, O Thuribor,
For Toby, too, to tread —
To sneak up on a swanky Elf
And bonk him on the head.'

'And I will, too,' said Toby, 'if I get half a chance! I'll have another nap until the sun gets up and then I'll be on his trail.'

The sun came up warm and bright and Toby swam across to the track and set off to shadow Elgrim. It was easy going, for Thuribor had made a good job of clearing the way. Toby meant to get up close enough to

Here is Elgrim, sending the magic Thuribor ahead of him to clear a path through the forest. According to the Elves, trees will always get out of your way if you axe them properly.

Elgrim to see when the Elf turned aside from the path to rest after his night-long hike.

What Toby would do then he hadn't quite decided – whether it would be better to sneak past the sleeping Elgrim and put as many miles between them as he could, or to carry out his first idea of bonking him on the head. Toby rather favoured bonking and that raised the question of *what* to bonk *with* and *how*, exactly, to bonk.

He ploughed on, lost in thought about this matter when suddenly . . . *he found himself walking into a great, prickly, holly-bush*! Toby jumped back and looked around in alarm. The clear pathway that Thuribor had cut went right up to the holly-bush – and there it stopped.

Toby scouted on either side of the path but he could find no sign of a track. What had happened to Elgrim? The Elf must be on another path. But how to find it?

'Only one thing to do,' Toby told himself. 'Get up a tree – as high up as I can – and spy out the land from above.'

So Toby chose the tallest tree he could see and he shinned up as high as he could and he stared this way and that until his eyes ached but not a glimpse of a path could he see. If only there was some sign of movement down there . . . or even the faintest whisper of the Elf's marching song to guide him.

'Oh, come on, Elgrim!' snorted Toby impatiently. 'Where the blazes have you got to?'

'I'm down here,' said the voice of Elgrim!

The Elf was standing near the foot of the tree, swinging his axe in one hand and jigging about from one foot to the other in evil glee, having led Toby into a trap.

'Oh, er, good morning,' said Toby. 'Nice day.'

'Good morning,' answered Elgrim. 'Come down, please. I'm going to kill you.'

'You come up here, then, and try!' said Toby. 'If you can find your feet behind all those whiskers.'

'I don't need to climb up there,' snapped the Elf,

'— and you leave my whiskers alone! All I have to do is to send my magic axe, Thuribor, to deal with you. One word from me and it will fly up there and slice your silly head off.'

Toby was searching frantically in his mind for some plan of escape. In the meantime he kept up a bold front.

'You've forgotten, Elgrim, that it's daytime now, and Elves haven't any magic in daylight! Magic axe, my foot! It's only an ordinary chopper now!' *And as soon as he had uttered those words, Toby realised he had made a fatal mistake.*

'An ordinary chopper!' answered Elgrim, with a roar of laughter. 'Why that's just what it is – and thank you for reminding me! An *ordinary* chopper is all I need to cut down that tree. An *ordinary* chopper is all I need to chop your foolish head off when you come crashing down with it!'

And with his wild war-whoop of '*Elgrim elohi elohiri*!' the sturdy Elf sent his axe biting deep into the trunk of the tree.

CHAPTER 16

DAVID BECOMES A DOCTOR

WHEN the boys parted, David decided to push ahead through the night as fast as he could. His idea was to get as near as possible to Black Walter's rearguard, stalk them, and then circle around them when they stopped to rest. He could travel, he felt, much more quickly than a group of heavily-armed men. There would be time to rest when he had them well behind him.

The path climbed steadily through the forest and the going was easy until, an hour or so before dawn, a cold white mist rolled through the trees. The path became icy as well as difficult to see, so that David, after stumbling along for a long, long time, was cheered to see a sudden warm red glow right ahead.

'Thank goodness for the sun,' he thought. But a few moments later he realised he was wrong, for first he caught the smell of wood-smoke, then he heard the crackle of flames. And soon he could see the flames themselves, flames of a camp-fire, with the black silhouettes of helmeted men around it!

David dropped to the ground and crawled silently towards the encampment. A quick glimpse of the faces of the men confirmed his guess: the weird, tattooed patterns proved them to be the henchmen of Black Walter.

David crept closer until he was close enough to distinguish what they were saying.

'. . . millions, I tell you,' growled a deep voice. 'Millions to share among us! Once Black Walter has sold the Golden Cactus we'll never need to work again . . .'

'Don't count your chickens before they're hatched,' said a sour voice. 'He's only two stages ahead . . . and there's a long way to go before he gets to Castle Doom.'

'Listen to Wolfgang the Gloomy,' jeered someone. 'What's to *stop* the Baron reaching Castle Doom? People run even at the sound of his name. Anyway, Redbeard and The Fox are with him. An army would flee before the three of them!'

'You're an ass,' answered the sour voice. 'It's not Black Walter I worry about but the Golden Cactus itself. The air is freezing, man, and such plants need warmth. who knows what may happen to it if it should be nipped by frost?'

There was a moment's silence. Clearly this was something the villains had not thought of. But suddenly a harsh, commanding voice snapped out: 'So! We have a soldier who thinks his leader would not have the wit to guard against such a thing! A soldier who thinks his leader is a fool! Take that man and give him fifty lashes . . .'

David crawled away rapidly as the ground round the camp-fire broke up. Not until he was a hundred yards away, and the fire just a dim red glow, did he get to his feet and work his way to the forest track.

After some time the mist started to thin out and soon

pale sunlight – real sunlight this time – began to filter through the trees. With Black Walter's rearguard behind him, David strode ahead humming merrily. Until he came up with the evil Baron himself, he felt he was out of danger.

So, humming away, he didn't hear a movement in the trees ahead of him. He didn't notice a strange stirring of leaves on a branch that overhung his path.

And so he was taken completely by surprise when a heavy figure in black chain-mail dropped on him from the sky and David found himself lying flat on his back with the point of a sword at his throat.

'Better lie quite still,' warned the black warrior. He stooped to pick up David's cap and his eyes glowed with greed as he fingered the golden letters on the front of it. 'Get up,' he said, stuffing the cap under his tunic. 'Turn round – and march!' And with the sword-point pricking between his shoulder-blades, David found himself going back along the path.

In a few minutes he would be thrust before the Captain of Black Walter's rearguard. In those few minutes he had to think up a plan that would save him from their clutches and – if possible – bring him nearer to the Golden Cactus itself. In his mind he went over the talk that he had heard among the soldiers, and suddenly a wild idea came into his head. It seemed crazy, but . . .

'Forward scout reporting,' roared his guard. 'I bring a prisoner.' And he thrust David into the circle of soldiers who thronged around him threateningly. The Captain clinked forward to question him but before he could speak, David yelled furiously: 'Is this the way you treat your master's friends? I shall have much to tell Black Walter when we meet!'

The Captain, who had intended to have some sport with his prisoner, fell back a pace. His jaw dropped.

'Call off this dog of yours that dared to lay hands on me!' ranted David. 'How much longer am I to be kept from the Baron's side by a tongue-tied idiot? Well? Speak, man!' David roared this out so loudly that the Captain jumped a foot in the air.

'But-but, sir . . .' he stuttered.

'Orders were sent to you to provide me with a horse . . . instead I am met by a cut-throat who leaps on me from a tree. How long do you think that the Golden Cactus can live in this freezing weather without the aid of a cactus doctor? Eh?'

'But, noble sir, how was the scout to recognize you . . . ?' The Captain at last managed to get a few words in.

'Recognize me?! Seize that thieving scout of yours and take my cap from under his tunic.

'There!' cried David, as his cap was handed over to the Captain, 'Can your men not read? Do they not know that only the highest officials proclaim their rank in letters of gold? And you – surely *you* know what these letters stand for?' And David pointed to the letters C.C. on the cap.

The Captain licked his dry lips. 'Oh, yes, er . . . surely . . .' he began.

'Quite right!' said David. 'What else could it be but "*Chief Conservator*"? I am Chief Conservator of the State Cactus Conservatory. Who else would the Baron call to his aid?'

David snatched his cap from the Captain's hands, jammed it on his head and glared around him.

'I have no time to waste on fools!' he snapped. 'A horse – at once! If this delay brings any sickness upon the Golden Cactus, you will lose your heads – the lot of you!'

But already the Captain was yelling for a horse to be saddled . . . 'The swiftest we have . . .' The men were milling around David, pressing gifts upon him . . .

'Take this warm cape, noble sir!'

'Honour me by accepting this sword, revered Doctor.'

David took the gifts gladly, for a new idea had come into his head . . . a breath-taking idea. He flung himself into the saddle, set spurs to the black stallion, and thundered off along the forest trail.

His goal was the Baron's camp. He was determined to match his wits with Black Walter – face to face.

CHAPTER 17

TOBY SELLS A JEWEL

TOBY'S tree shuddered under the blows of Thuribor and he realised that it was only a matter of minutes before it would come crashing to the ground. Then, even if he was not killed by the fall, he could not escape the Elf's murderous axe.

If only he had a weapon! If only there was something he could throw at the Elf and stun him long enough to shin down the tree and dash for the safety of the island! He plunged his hand in his pocket and his fingers closed round the stone – David's souvenir from the Howling Valley. No: that was too small. He felt the smooth roundness of the glass marble and, as he fingered it, a plan began to shape in his mind.

Toby pulled the marble from his pocket and looked at it. It really was a super-marble – a perfect sphere of purest crystal – and as he turned it around between his fingers, the sun's rays rebounded from it in lightning flashes of blinding white light.

The axe blows stopped suddenly.

'What have you got there?' called the Elf.

'A gift for you, if you'll spare my life,' answered Toby. 'You've never in your life seen a jewel like this!' And he twisted the crystal sphere this way and that so that it flashed fire.

'Throw it down so that I can examine it,' said Elgrim craftily.

'Oh, no! You don't catch me that way!' answered Toby and he kept the marble turning and flashing while Elgrim stared in envy.

Toby had wondered if he could excite the Elf's greed so much that he would scurry after the marble if Toby threw it some distance away. This would give him the chance to make a dash for freedom – but it would be a very slim chance.

But now, while he turned the marble in his fingers, Toby noticed something else. As he held it out temptingly over Elgrim's upturned face, he saw that it threw a small white circle of light on the Elf's beard. It gave him a new and exciting idea.

'If you don't throw the jewel to me, I shall take it from you anyway, when the tree comes crashing down!' said Elgrim.

'But if I throw it far out into the undergrowth you may never find it – whether you kill me or not,' answered Toby. 'Why not accept my offer? My life in exchange for this priceless jewel. See how beautiful it is!'

'I would like to see it closer,' said the Elf.

'Very well then . . . look!' said Toby, and he reached down towards Elgrim, carefully focusing the circle of sunlight until it shrank to a burning point of light at the bottom of the Elf's long beard.

'Closer!' cried Elgrim, his voice hoarse with desire. He dropped his axe and reached up with both hands, trying to seize the glittering prize.

And at that moment, with a crackle and a *whoosh*, his great long bushy beard burst into flames!'

'Aaaah!' screeched Elgrim, leaping about in panic. 'Help! Help! Fire! Water! Bring water!'

'The river . . .!' Toby shouted. 'Run to the river!'

Elgrim needed no second telling. Trailing flames and smoke and the smell of burning whiskers, he plunged back down the track towards the water.

And Toby? Another, even better, idea had just struck him. He slithered down the tree at top speed, grabbed Thuribor, and set off after the Elf.

Elgrim, screeching madly, couldn't have heard it if there'd been an elephant behind him – and he couldn't have cared either. All he wanted to do was to get to the river's edge and dunk his blazing beard in the water.

He got there at record speed. He flung himself on all fours at the water's edge and down went his head amid a great hissing and rolling white clouds of steam.

Toby arrived behind him at that moment. Shouting the Elf's own war-cry, '*Elgrim elohi elohiri*!' he placed a foot firmly behind the stooping Elf, shot him head-first into the river, and dived in after him.

'Uggle-blug!' spluttered Elgrim as his soot-blackened face came above water.

'Don't understand you,' giggled Toby and pushed him under again. 'Just long enough to take any fight out of you,' he added, and he turned on his back, grabbed the Elf under the chin, and towed him to the island.

He propped him limply against a tree. But Toby remembered how swiftly Elgrim had recovered from his last ducking so he fished out the piece of string from his pocket, pulled the Elf's arms round the trunk of the tree behind him, and bound his wrists firmly together.

Elgrim was a sad sight. The flames from his beard had burned the toe-caps off his boots, the front of his tunic was blackened and below his sooty face – from which two reddened eyes now opened in a glare of hatred – only about two inches of charred and soggy beard remained.

'Don't kill me!' pleaded the Elf weakly, eyeing the axe Thuribor, which Toby was idly swinging. 'Let me go and I'll . . . I'll give you Thuribor.'

'Well, I like your cheek!' said Toby. 'I've *got* Thuribor. But I don't want it and I'm going to make sure that you don't have it, either. So watch . . .' And Toby hurled the axe into the deepest part of the river.

'If you want Thuribor, you can swim for it,' he said.

'You know I can't swim,' growled Elgrim.

'I certainly do,' laughed Toby, – 'and that's why I'm leaving you on this island. Good-bye, Elgrim!' And Toby turned to go.

'You wait!' snarled the Elf. 'My magic returns when the sun goes down. I will escape, somehow. And when we meet again . . . *aaarrrr*! glub-glub . . . *glob-glub-glob*!'

Elgrim uttered these very strange sounds because Toby had suddenly pushed the glass marble into his mouth.

'I promised you my wonderful jewel if my life was

spared,' remarked Toby. 'So there it is – and mind you don't swallow it!' Then he dived into the water and swam ashore.

Before he rejoined the track among the trees he turned for one last look at the castaway. Elgrim was struggling furiously with his bonds and his mouth was moving angrily. Toby felt it was a good thing he could not hear what the Elf was trying to say.

Toby strode happily along. He soon found the holly-bush where the track had appeared to stop and, working around it, he eventually found the way again. It was still early in the morning and he could put many miles between himself and Elgrim before nightfall brought magic to aid the Elf's escape.

It was not until late in the afternoon that Toby stopped . . . and this wasn't because he was tired. It was because he noticed some familiar-looking plants in a clearing beside the path. He moved closer and studied them and in no time at all Toby was ferreting about among them at top-speed.

As you've most likely guessed, it was the presence of something to eat that had attracted him . . . not merely *food* (which can mean anything, even cold tapioca pudding), but a delicacy of which Toby is especially fond: wild raspberries.

He picked them, he sat and he *gorged*. (Yes, he did gorge. In fact, he *gobbled*, and there's no denying it.) He ate and he rested and he thought with pleasure of the way he had beaten Elgrim the Elf. And then he looked over what remained of his five 'weapons' – one pocket-knife, one piece of chewing-gum, and the stone that David had given him.

Two 'weapons' had been used – and Toby reckoned they had been well used. After all, to beat a wily old Elf and his magic axe with nothing more dangerous than a glass marble and a piece of string . . . well, that was pretty good going. Toby flicked away a tiny red ant that was crawling over the stone, and put the things back in his pocket.

His plan was to push on until just before sunset and then to find a comfortable perch in a tree that was well away from the trail, and have a much-needed sleep. He decided, however, that he could afford time for a short nap before tackling the next lap of his journey, so he lay down and closed his eyes.

But Toby was never to have that snooze.

A sudden loud stirring in the undergrowth aroused him. He opened his eyes in alarm and looked up.

High above him, and looking as though it was hanging from enormous supports like the legs of a giant crane, was a horrifying face. Great black horns waved above two enormous eyes that glowed redly as they glared down on him. And below those eyes he could see nothing but teeth . . . teeth that clashed together hungrily as the great head swung down towards him.

With a cry of terror Toby sprang to his feet and fled wildly through the twilit forest with the devilish Thing at his heels.

CHAPTER 18

DAVID IN THE LION'S DEN

An hour or so after leaving the camp of the black warriors, David stopped to rest his horse – and himself – work out a plan of campaign and have a nap. He decided after long thought that if he could fool Black Walter into letting him take care of the Golden Cactus, it would be quite enough to be going on with. After that, it would be a case of waiting and watching for a chance to make off with it. If he was questioned about his knowledge of cactuses and how to keep them in good health, well, he'd have to bluff his way through. After all, though David knew next to nothing about such plants, he was pretty certain that the Black Baron and his henchmen knew even less.

So he mounted again and, lying low in the saddle,

urged the black stallion to a gallop. The powerful beast seemed to fly over the track and when, towards evening, David saw a horseman facing him on the road ahead, he knew he must be nearing Black Walter's camp.

The horseman swung alongside, keeping pace with him.

'Whither?' he shouted.

'To Black Walter's side!' shouted David over the thunder of their hooves. He pointed to the letters on his cap and gave the title he'd invented for himself. 'I have been called to help in case the weather should bring sickness to the Golden Cactus,' he added. 'It cannot bear the cold.'

'The Baron rode through a freezing fog on these slopes last night,' the man replied. 'We shall both lose our heads if you arrive too late. There is a shorter way to the camp. Follow me. We stop for no one!'

For two hours they rode at breakneck pace along a trail invisible to David and so rough that it was all he could do to keep his seat.

Several times he heard his companion roar out some password and caught a glimpse of another black warrior reining back his horse as they thundered past.

At last, smothered in dust and with aching arms, they clattered to a halt in Black Walter's camp and mail-clad warriors rushed to take their horses as David's companion shouted instructions.

'Come!' he ordered David, and led him over to a large tent that stood apart from those of the small, picked force of soldiers who made up the Baron's household.

At a curt word of command the guards at the entrance to the tent pulled back the black canvas flap and David and his companion stepped inside and halted.

A harsh voice snapped irritably: 'Well? What is it?'

'The Cactus Doctor is here at the Baron's request!'

The man stood to one side to let David come forward, and as he did so he found himself looking into the face of Black Walter, the fabled Baron of Bunkulm.

There could be no doubt as to who it was: no other man could look so evil. The Baron was seated at a heavy

A tense moment for David, under questioning by the evil Black Walter. The villain on the left is The Fox. You'll notice he's testing the point of his sword by pressing it on his own finger. He isn't very bright, really.

oaken table, arms folded, head pushed forward suspiciously. His black chain-mail glinted in the flickering light of a brazier and his black-plumed helmet lay beside him.

His great dome of a head was completely bald, but, like his square, brutal face, it was covered with a black tracery of tattooing. He had a heavy black moustache and a black spade-beard. But it was his eyes that made the face so fearsome. They were a tawny yellow, like those of a wild animal, and at this moment they were fixed unwinkingly on David.

'So?' he said. 'Could I have forgotten?' He shot a glance at a man who sat on his right, a red-bearded warrior whose lips seemed set in a permanent sneer. 'Did I ask *you* to send for this person, Redbeard?' he asked.

'Nay!' answered the other. 'What would *I* know of doctors and such-like bookish fools? Maybe you asked The Fox to send for him?'

The soldier at the other end of the table, a man with a thin face and long nose, shook his head.

'So!' said Black Walter again. '*You* did not . . . and *he* did not . . .' And suddenly he roared, in a frightening voice: 'And *I* certainly did not send for you! Then who did? And who are you?'

David snapped back. 'If you'd given me a chance to speak I would have told you . . .'

'Ha! The little man shows spirit!' said Black Walter. 'You have your chance now. Speak.'

'It was the Captain of your rearguard who called me,' said David. 'He is my cousin. *I* am – as you can see from these letters that show my rank,' (he pointed to his cap) '— I am Chief Conservator of the State Cactus Conservatory. Last night there was a freezing fog along the route to this camp and my cousin remembered what I have often told him – *a cactus that catches a chill may die within hours. That* is why he sent for me and told me to ride here at top speed.'

The Baron was startled. 'By thunder!' he cried, bringing his fist down on the table with a crash. 'If the Golden Cactus has . . .'

'Oh, rubbish!' laughed Redbeard. 'We wrapped it up well enough.'

'*You* wrapped it up well enough?' David said. 'And just what do *you* know about such matters? Are you not aware that *Notocactus leninghausii* is a most delicate plant?' (David has a wonderful memory for any curious words that he has read and this was one that he'd seen under a picture of some cactus plants. He hadn't the faintest idea which one it stood for.*)

'Me aware of *what*?' said Redbeard rudely. 'Really, the things this fellow says are all Greek to me!'

Black Walter was silent, watching the two of them and wrestling with his suspicions.

But now The Fox spoke. 'Of course it's all Greek to you, Redbeard,' he said nastily, 'because the gentleman was speaking *Latin*.'

He turned to the Baron.

'We can take no chances,' he said. 'The Doctor here has endured great discomfort to come to our aid. He must see The Golden Cactus at once. We have been wasting valuable time.'

'Aye, that we have,' growled Black Walter, and he turned a baleful eye on Redbeard. 'Go with The Fox, learned Doctor,' he said to David. 'Examine the Golden Cactus with the greatest care . . .'

David nodded and The Fox took his arm in friendly fashion to lead him from the tent.

'. . . And, Doctor!' called Black Walter as they reached the doorway. If you find any sickness in the Golden Cactus, you will cure it. You will cure it, my little Doctor, for if the Golden Cactus dies – then so do you!'

'Aye,' shouted Redbeard. 'And we'll see to it that you have a painful death – in Greek *or* in Latin!'

The Fox hurried David along until they came to a small, square tent, ringed by armed men.

'Do not fear Redbeard,' said The Fox, putting his hand on David's shoulder. 'He is an ignorant fool.

* David's memory didn't let him down. There *is* a cactus with that odd name, and it's quite a delicate one, too. Strangely enough, it is also known as the Golden Ball Cactus.

We – you and I – are men of learning. Between us . . .' He stopped suddenly. 'But there will be time enough to talk when your task is done,' he added, thrusting him into the tent.

And as David stumbled forward, a sudden white brilliance struck him like a blow in the face and he flung up his hand to shade his eyes.

A few feet in front of him the stolen cactus glowed with a blinding golden radiance. It was within his grasp at last!

CHAPTER 19

TOBY TAKES UP COOKERY

TOBY, chased by the monster, was managing to keep ahead of it – though only just ahead. But soon he realised that it was gaining on him. Across his path he saw a wide gap in the ground where a stream had cut out a deep channel. He called up all his strength and leaped across, but a moment later he heard the scraping of the monster's legs as it scrambled up the steep bank behind him and came snorting at his heels again.

Toby felt his strength failing and he realised there was only one thing he could do. And so, once more, he found himself up a tree.

For the first time he now had a chance to get a good look at the creature and he realised with horror that it was an *ant* – but an ant that can never have been seen in the world before.

It was as big as the biggest St Bernard dog and its huge red body swung high above the ground on its six enormous legs. The horns that Toby had glimpsed were really long antennae and they waved in anger as the Giant Ant reared up against the tree. It rolled its saucer-like eyes and champed its sharp fangs as it looked at him hungrily in the gathering gloom.

Toby settled himself firmly on his perch and broke off a nearby branch.

'If you try to get up here,' he told the Giant Ant, 'I'll bonk you – good and proper!' They were bold words, but I can tell you that Toby was feeling anything but brave at that moment.

The Giant Ant, however, had no intention of climbing after him. It just stood there, clasping the tree, with its head almost halfway up the trunk, as if it had been frozen. But its eyes never closed and they never left Toby's face. The creature realised that it had only to wait.

As Toby studied it he suddenly realised that it was exactly like the tiny red ant that he had knocked off David's souvenir of Howling Valley – the stone that he called the Shaggy Dog stone, the stone of the kind that the great beasts of Howling Valley licked hungrily whenever they could find it.

Perhaps that was the secret of Howling Valley! Perhaps it was the constant licking of the stones that made the creatures in the valley so enormous. And perhaps that was why the Giant Ant was pursuing him – to get at the stone again.

If it managed to get *another* lick . . .! Toby wedged himself tightly in the fork of the tree and closed his eyes. Somehow he had to get through the night and hope that daylight would bring him an idea of how to escape.

Right now Toby couldn't see how the three 'weapons' he had in his pocket could help him. He'd never be able to drive the blade of a pocket-knife through the Giant Ant's hide – and what earthly use was a piece of chewing-gum? As for the Shaggy Dog stone . . . 'That,' Toby told himself, 'seems to me more like an anti-*boy* weapon. But I won't throw it away yet – perhaps David can think up some use for it.'

Well, as you know, nothing can stop a sleepy boy from sleeping – not even a Giant Ant – and Toby did at last doze off. Dreams of ants as big as horses woke him from time to time and when he looked down he saw the eyes of the monster fixed firmly on him.

Daylight came at last with Toby wondering just how long the Giant Ant could keep on staring at him without blinking, when . . . it actually *did* blink! It blinked, then turned its head to one side and looked towards the track. It seemed to have heard something and, after a few moments, Toby heard the sound too.

It was the noise of a horse cantering. Then suddenly, not far down the trail that he had come along, Toby caught a glimpse of a black helmet, then a black-tattooed face. It was one of Black Walter's warriors on patrol.

The Giant Ant swung round and dropped to its feet – all six of them – and began to move stealthily towards the cover of a bush beside the track. Maddened by hunger, it must have felt that here was an easier prey than a boy up a tree.

For Toby, the beast's move raised a big problem. Here was an enemy coming along who would certainly slay Toby if he could. And here was a beast that could kill that enemy, giving Toby a chance to escape. All he had to do was to keep quiet and his foe would ride right into the jaws of the Giant Ant.

What *did* Toby do? Why, he did what you would do, I'm sure: he took a deep breath as the black warrior neared the beast's ambush and he yelled: '*Look out*! *Danger*!'

The soldier swung round, looking towards the sound and drawing his sword in one swift movement. And as he did so the Giant Ant leaped right over the bush and fell upon him, biting and clawing. At the sight of the hideous attacker, the soldier's horse whinnied in terror, reared, throwing him from the saddle, and bolted up the trail. The man's sword flew from his hand and fell close to the foot of Toby's tree.

Toby didn't stop to think of danger. Down he went in a flying leap. He seized the sword, raised it above his head and advanced with a yell upon the Giant Ant. At the sudden sound behind it, the beast raised its head. At once Toby swept the sword in a great, gleaming circle and – *that* was the end of the monster that had wanted to make a meal of him.

The black warrior scrambled painfully to his feet. He was badly shaken but his helmet and chain-mail had saved him from serious hurt. He came with arm outstretched to Toby, grasped his hand and gripped it strongly.

'Sandor thanks you, comrade,' he said. 'But now, alas, I have my duty to fulfil. I must ask you who you are and whither you go. And if you do not give me fair answer then my orders are to slay you.' With a quick movement he snatched his sword from Toby's grasp. 'Speak now, friend – and may your words ring true!'

When you're in a tight corner like that you have to think quickly. Toby tried to, but he wasn't getting along very well when Sandor himself put an idea into his head.

'Come,' he said, 'tell me first what mean these letters?' and he pointed to Toby's cap. *Ping*! went a little bell in Toby's head and he knew just what to do.

'Why,' he said, 'you must be a new recruit to our master's service not to know that! "C.C." means that I am Chief Cook in the kitchen of Black Walter. You *must* be new,' Toby went on, 'I have not seen you before.'

'I have not yet been inside Castle Doom,' said Sandor. 'Nor have I tasted your dishes in Castle Terror either. I am no newcomer to the Baron's service, but my task is to patrol the forest ways and guard them against his enemies. How I would like to eat under a roof, for once!'

Toby guessed that Castle Terror must be another of Black Walter's strongholds, so he said: 'It is Castle Terror that I come from. I am called to Castle Doom. There is to be a great feast when the Golden Cactus gets safely there. Come to my kitchen, Sandor. I will see that you have as fine a meal as they have in the Great Hall!'

This was a good move, for Sandor thanked him warmly, offering his help if ever Toby needed it.

'Perhaps,' said Toby, 'you could help me now I hoped to arrive at Castle Doom well ahead of the Baron. But that monster' – he pointed to the body of the Giant Ant – 'has eaten my horse. Since I must go on foot, is there a shorter way than by this track?'

'You shall have a horse, friend,' said Sandor, 'and I

will also show you a shorter way to Castle Doom. My horse will not have run far: he will come to my call.' He whistled shrilly and after a while they heard the clop-clop of hooves. Soon Sandor was patting the horse and calming its fears.

'You know, doubtless, that there is a river below us,' he told Toby. 'On the hillside across the river is the road that Black Walter himself is taking to the Castle. Go down in the valley and follow the river until you see a ridge ahead of you. Climb that ridge and you will see Castle Doom almost at your feet. You will be there long before our master. For me there is a weary walk ahead – so see that the meal you promised me is a good one!'

'I will,' said Toby, and set the horse's head towards the valley. He turned to ask a final question.

'When I get near to this ridge, how shall I recognise it?' he asked. 'Is there any landmark?'

'You will know it for certain,' replied Sandor, 'when you see a ruined tower.'

A ruined tower in sight of Castle Doom! Why, that was where he was to meet David! His lonely journey was ending at last. Very soon now, Toby was sure, the two of them would be together, laying their plans for the assault on Castle Doom!

But if he could have seen what was happening to David at that very moment he wouldn't have been sure of it at all.

CHAPTER 20

DAVID SCORES A KNOCK-OUT

IN the centre of a table the Golden Cactus stood in its bowl upon a large block of solid oak. Over it was a dome of glass, pierced with holes for ventilation, and over the glass was a cage of wrought iron with a hook on top.

The cage was fixed to the oaken block on each side by a hasp and staple, secured by strong iron locks.

David was thinking quickly as he went towards the Golden Cactus.

'Has it taken harm from the cold?' asked The Fox. 'If so, Redbeard will suffer for it. And without him,' added The Fox thoughtfully, 'there would be more to share among those who have done their duty well.'

Clearly The Fox wanted Redbeard out of the way and therefore he would like David to say that the Golden Cactus was in need of care. This suited David's plan, too. To say that the Golden Cactus had suffered on its journey would mean that he would be given the job of looking after it, and while he was doing that he felt sure he could think up a way of getting it out of Black Walter's grasp. Meanwhile, any trouble between the Baron's lieutenants would mean that Black Walter had less time to keep an eye on what David was up to.

So he said: 'I very much fear it was hurt by frost during the journey. It cannot have been well wrapped up.'

'I knew it!' said The Fox.

'I must open the case,' said David, 'and look at it closely. But first I must disinfect my breath, before I dare remove the cover.' David pulled the chewing-gum from his pocket and stuffed it in his mouth. A strong scent of peppermint filled the air.

'A powerful herb indeed,' marvelled The Fox, sniffing appreciatively.

'You have the keys?' asked David.

'Yes,' answered The Fox. 'I will open the case for you.'

'And endanger the plant with your polluted breath?' said David with a laugh. 'Nay, comrade! Hand me the keys. I will open it and give the case to you to hold while I make my examination.'

The Fox handed him the keys and David opened the locks and passed over the glass cover with the warning: 'Stand well back . . . and breathe lightly. This is a critical moment.'

David was now right in front of the Golden Cactus, cutting off the light from its radiant flowers so that Red Fox could not see his movements.

As David leaned forward pretending to examine the plant closely, he slipped the chewing gum from his mouth and pressed it between the two keys. Now he had a perfect copy of their shapes and he could make keys of his own to fit the locks.

He put the gum back in his pocket, drew out the glass marble hidden in the palm of his hand, and dropped it lightly on the soil behind the plant.

'The cactus will recover,' he said sharply, ' — but you have been near to disaster. I arrived only just in time. If it is left in my care I promise you many more golden blooms. Aye, and more of the crystal drops as well.'

The Fox was startled. 'Crystal drops?' he said, puzzled. 'Flowers of gold – I knew of these. But has this plant other wonders for us, then?'

'You mean you did not know of this?' asked David and he picked up the glass marble from behind the Golden Cactus. 'Look,' he said, and he turned it this way and that so that it caught the golden rays of the cactus flowers and glowed with fire.

'Let me touch it,' said The Fox hoarsely and reached out a trembling hand.

'Give me the cover of the cactus. I will hold it for you,' said David. 'Then you can take the crystal in both hands and examine it.'

The Fox took it and David could see the greed in his eyes as he watched the play of light and felt its smooth roundness.

'What *is* this wondrous jewel, doctor?' whispered The Fox.

'It is a thing of far more value to your master than all the golden flowers of that plant put together,' said David. 'Whoever carries a crystal drop from the Golden Cactus cannot be harmed by any weapon of steel, however sharp its blade or edge may be. Arrows and spears glance off him, swords shatter when they touch his body.'

'Aaah!' breathed The Fox. 'A greater prize than gold indeed. And I did not know . . . I did not know.'

'How strange!' said David. 'I felt certain that *you* would know this thing. I am sure that Black Walter knows it.'

'Aye,' growled The Fox angrily. 'Aye, I wager he does!'

David said briskly: 'Well, my examination is finished. The Baron will be anxious for my report. Let us replace the crystal drop – it may have grown a little larger by the time we reach Castle Doom – and cover the Golden Cactus.' And he walked towards the cactus and began to lower the iron-covered dome over it.

The Fox strode hastily to the other side of the table so that he faced David. 'The crystal came from this side, didn't it?' he asked and when David nodded, The Fox passed a hand under the dome. 'There,' he said, 'It is safely back again. Put down the cover.'

But David knew well what had happened, and while The Fox was turning the heavy keys in the locks he stole a quick glance round the back of the Golden Cactus. The wonder-working 'crystal drop' was no longer there.

The Fox strode into Black Walter's tent with David behind him.

'The doctor guarantees the *future* health of the Golden Cactus,' he declared. 'But he says he arrived only in the nick of time. The cactus was sick. And the reason for this was that it had not been properly protected on the journey. I accuse Redbeard of failing in his duty.'

'I deny it!' roared Redbeard, leaping to his feet, sword in hand.

'Liar,' answered The Fox.

'Hold!' shouted Black Walter. 'Come and sit beside me, little Doctor, and you shall see how soldiers decide who is in the right or wrong.' And as David took his seat, Black Walter said: 'And now – set to!'

At once The Fox flung himself on his opponent and

Redbeard found himself being forced back against the wall of the tent.

'I have never seen The Fox seek battle before,' muttered Black Walter. 'He is the wary one – a man who works by stealth. Redbeard is the swordsman – but look at him now!'

For Redbeard was panting. He was puzzled by the foolhardiness of the other's attack.

Black Walter saw the sudden fear in Redbeard's eyes and he roared with laughter.

'Oh, bravo The Fox!' he shouted. 'A warrior at last!'

At the shout Redbeard turned his head for a moment. Only a moment – but it was enough. The Fox struck him lifeless to the ground.

Then he turned to Black Walter.

'And now,' he cried, 'now, liar . . . deceiver . . . it is your turn to die! The Golden Cactus, with all its marvels, shall be mine alone!'

In one bound Black Walter had leaped over the table. Sword in hand he faced The Fox.

'You are mad,' he said quietly, 'and I will have no madmen in my service.'

The Fox laughed triumphantly. 'You cannot harm me,' he taunted, and he flew at his master, waving his weapon crazily. 'Your sword will shatter if it even touches me!'

'That we shall see,' grunted Black Walter – and slew The Fox with one mighty blow.

Then he turned to David.

'From now on,' he said, 'the Golden Cactus is in your care, little Doctor. You will live beside it. You will sleep beside it. Food will be sent to you. If you need to open the case to give treatment to the cactus you will send for me, for I mean to keep the keys in my hands. Strange things have happened in this camp since you came, little Doctor, and I am a suspicious man. Remember what I have already told you: if the Golden Cactus dies, you die with it. Now go to your post.'

Inside the tent where the Golden Cactus stood, David sat on the bed they had placed for him and set himself to think furiously. So far his plan had been a marvellous success. Two very dangerous men had been removed from his path. The next step, his escape, was much more difficult but he felt sure that before the night was over the Golden Cactus would no longer be resting in Black Walter's camp.

The same idea, however, was in the mind of someone else.

CHAPTER 21

TOBY WATCHES A HOLE

DAVID'S first move was to make himself some keys so that he could remove the Golden Cactus from its heavy cage. His bed was a rough affair, just a raised frame of saplings with thinner branches laid across it and covered with straw. He carefully selected one of the small branches and, taking out his pocket-knife, started on the lengthy job of carving a couple of keys to match the impression of the real ones that he had made in the chewing-gum.

His plan was a daring one. When the keys were ready he would call for a brazier containing a hot fire of charcoal, on the excuse that the temperature was getting too low for the cactus to be safe. After that he would remove the cactus from its case, wrap it carefully in his cape and then make a pile of the straw and the wood from his bed all along the front part of the tent. A few glowing pieces of charcoal would quickly start a furious fire and, as everyone ran to the blaze, David would cut a hole through the canvas at the rear of the tent and, keeping in the shadows, get his horse and lead it quietly through the forest to a point on the road that led to Castle Doom.

When Black Walter found he had been tricked, David was sure that he would believe the Golden Cactus was on its way back to Blumendorf. Certainly he would never for a moment imagine that the thief was riding towards Castle Doom. So Black Walter would go pounding off in the wrong direction while David would make his way comfortably to the ruined tower that overlooked Castle Doom, pick up Toby, and together they would return by a roundabout way to the House of Cobwebb and from there to Blumendorf.

By the time David had finished the keys midnight was long past. The whole camp slept, but David had never felt more awake and alert. He stood up and stretched himself. This was the moment for swift action.

But it was the moment, too, when he first heard the music.

It was soft and gentle and slow. It did not come from outside. It seemed to be in the tent itself. It was a strange melody, like none he had ever in his life heard, played on instruments that were not of this world. It seemed to draw all the strength from his limbs. He sat heavily on the bed. He could not struggle against his growing weakness. He felt tired – so very tired. His head fell back on the pillow. His eyes closed. All his wonderful plan was forgotten. He was sound asleep.

David woke suddenly. The camp was astir. The warriors must have been up hours ago for he could hear them drilling. The sun was high. Black Walter might come in at any moment to ask for his report on the condition of the Golden Cactus. The Golden Cactus that should long ago have been on the road to the ruined tower!

With cold gripping his heart, David turned over and leaped from the bed. The Golden Cactus was no longer in the tent. With the locked cage that had held it, it had disappeared. A round, gaping hole in the floor told David the terrible truth: Elgrim the Elf had taken the prize at leisure while David lay in a swoon brought on by his magic.

David ran to the table. There, scratched on the surface, was Elgrim's crow of triumph. David spelled out the clumsy lettering.

YOU FOOL (read the message)
THE GOLDEN CACTUS IS MINE.
–ELGRIM.

What was he to do? It was death to stay and face the anger of Black Walter. It might well be death if he went down the hole. But Elgrim had gone that way and where Elgrim was, there also was the Golden Cactus.

There was nothing for it but to follow the Elf. 'But first,' David told himself, 'it would be useful to have Black Walter chasing Elgrim – who pretended to be a friend of his – rather than have him on *my* trail.'

He took out his knife and carefully scratched in another two words so that Elgrim's message now read: –

YOU FOOL, BLACK WALTER!
THE GOLDEN CACTUS IS MINE.
–ELGRIM.

Then he went to the edge of the hole. It yawned, black and deep, and measured very little more across than the width of David's shoulders.

He stood on the rim, raised his arms above his head and took a deep breath.

'Here I come, Elgrim!' he said and, dropping into the hole, he plummeted down, down, into the darkness and whatever might lie in wait for him below.

Far across the valley, in the bright sunlight, Toby jogged happily on Sandor's horse towards his goal – the ruined tower that now stood out clearly on the ridge ahead.

The ridge blocked the end of the valley and from its rocky face spouted the stream that flowed down the valley – the stream that washed around an island on which Toby had left Elgrim the Elf tied to a tree.

Toby chuckled at the thought and then looked again across to the cluster of black tents on the skyline opposite. Black Walter's troops, no doubt, thought Toby, and he wondered whether David would have managed to get safely past them and, if so, if he might find him already waiting at the ruined tower.

Then his eyes moved down towards the stream again and suddenly he said: 'Oho, what's this?' and slipping from his horse, he tethered it behind a clump of trees and peered across the valley.

What had caught his attention was a sudden gleam of light from the centre of a black hole part way up the hillside and partly screened by some bushes. There was a pile of fresh earth around the hole. 'But I can't imagine what kind of animal made that hole,' mused Toby. 'It's too big for a rabbit, too big for a fox, even. On the other hand, it's too small for a bear. And there's that flash again and . . . *what* a light!'

For there was a second gleam at the mouth of the hole that was brighter even than the bright sunshine – a flashing light that left the shade of the bushes and bobbed and danced across the hillside.

'Somebody's carrying it – whatever it is,' Toby told himself. Then, suddenly, as the bearer of the flashing light turned his head, Toby almost shouted with surprise.

'It's Elgrim, Elgrim!' he said. 'And if that's Elgrim then the light must come from the Golden Cactus. He must have stolen it from Black Walter. And I'm going to get it back,' declared Toby, and he swung round to untether his horse.

But before he could do so there was the blare of a trumpet from the black knot of tents high above the fleeing Elf. A score of black warriors, on horse and on foot, came plunging down the hillside towards Elgrim. A keen-eyed sentry had seen him and raised the alarm.

'*Now* what will he do?' asked Toby.

But there was only one thing that Elgrim *could* do, if he was to stay alive – and that was to put down the Golden Cactus and run. Run he did: Toby had never seen anyone move so quickly. Meanwhile, Black Walter's men – horse and foot-soldiers alike – ignored the scurrying Elf and made towards the blazing radiance of the Golden Cactus. It was only as they turned to bear it back up the hillside, cheering and slapping each other on the back, that a small group of horsemen moved aside to follow the trail of Elgrim. But he was nowhere to be seen and they had little heart for the chase now that the treasure had been recovered. So, very soon, they followed their comrades back to the camp.

'If Elgrim has any sense,' Toby said to himself, 'he'll

get underground and stay there for a long time. But what a tunneller he must be . . .' and Toby looked again at the hole in the hillside from which Elgrim had emerged with the Golden Cactus. And as he looked something shot out of the hole, rolled headlong down the steep grassy slope and ended up in the stream with a great splash.

But by that time, Toby, who had seen the colour of the uniform that 'something' wore, and had also noted the gleam of the gold lettering on the 'something's' cap, was standing on the bank and holding out a stout branch from a tree.

'Oh, hello, David,' he said casually. 'Fancy meeting you!'

The two boys sat beneath the trees and told each other of their adventures. David said that he had got stuck in Elgrim's tunnel and it took hours to free himself – then, when he did, he came tumbling out on to the hillside all in a heap.

'It was probably the sound of your struggles that scared Elgrim and sent him running into the open,' said Toby.

Then they discussed the stones from Howling Valley and the effect that Toby's stone had on the red ant. 'I think these stones are a danger to us, rather than a help,' Toby said. 'The only way I can think of using them would be to make ourselves into giants.'

'And then we'd be much easier targets for spears and arrows and things,' answered David. 'No, I don't think that would be a good idea at all.'

'Well, let's throw them away, then,' said Toby.

'And get ourselves chased by giant ants?'

'Chuck them in the river . . .'

'And then we might get eaten by giant frogs.'

'Seems silly to hang on to something that's no use to us.'

'Maybe . . . but let's keep them in our pockets,' said David. And then he used the argument that everybody uses from time to time. 'You never know,' he said, ' – they *might* come in handy – some time or another.'

By now the sun was shining directly on Black Walter's camp and the boys' side of the valley was in dark shadow.

So, feeling safe from observation by the camp sentinels, they mounted Sandor's horse and ambled comfortably along until they came to the ridge and the entrance to the ruined tower. They tethered the horse and went inside.

The tower had just one room, with a stone staircase that went up to the remains of an upper room – now roofless and with broken walls around it.

They pushed open the heavy oaken door of the lower room and went over to a slit window that gave them their first view of Black Walter's stronghold. The sight of it sent their hearts right down into their boots.

Far below stretched the seething, steaming waters of Boiling Lake. And in the centre of it, on a great pinnacle of jagged rock, the tall black turrets of Castle Doom pierced the shifting white clouds of steam and stood out, harsh and forbidding, against the treeless mountains beyond.

'However are we going to get in there – alive?' whispered David.

'And if we do, however are we going to get *out* of there – alive?' asked Toby.

The silence that followed that remark was broken by a resounding blow on the oaken door behind them and, as they swung round, it began slowly to open.

CHAPTER 22

ELGRIM MAKES A STRANGE BARGAIN

In the open doorway stood – Elgrim the Elf.

He looked a pitiful figure, with his charred fringe of whiskers, his tunic torn and earth-stained from his tunnelling, and his bare feet poking out where the toe-caps of his boots had been burned away.

'I come to offer a truce,' said the Elf.

'Nothing doing,' snapped David. 'We wouldn't trust you a yard, would we, Toby?'

'Not likely!' said Toby. 'And by the way, Elgrim, where's Thuribor?'

'You know well where it is,' growled Elgrim, '—on the river's bed and beyond my reach for I cannot swim nor can my magic reach through water. Now you know I am unarmed, why fear me?'

'We don't fear you,' said David. 'We just don't want anything to do with you.'

'You have no choice, I think,' said Elgrim. 'In an hour or so, Black Walter and his troops with the Golden Cactus will reach Boiling Lake, Among the rocks on the shore yonder is a bronze door which can be opened only from the inside. When the castle janitor unlocks the door, Black Walter and his men will pass down steep stairs to an underground tunnel that leads into Castle Doom. When all have passed, the door will be locked. Within the castle the pumps will be stopped and the passage will fill with the water of the lake. How, then, can you steal into the castle to take the Golden Cactus?'

'We could swim through the tunnel,' said Toby.

'In boiling water?' jeered Elgrim.

'Why bother about a tunnel?' asked David. 'We could make a boat or a raft out of reeds and float across at night.'

'Oh, brilliant!' roared the Elf. 'And since when did reeds grow in boiling water? And if you managed to make a boat or a raft of any sort, and landed on the rocks, how would you get into the castle when there is no door in its thick walls?'

The boys were silent at this.

'You see,' said Elgrim, 'we *must* have a truce. You do not know how to enter the castle. I know how to get inside but working alone it will be a long and weary task. You need my help: I need yours. What do you say?'

Toby said thoughtfully: 'You're thinking of a new tunnel, aren't you? So you need someone to carry the earth out of the shaft as you dig it.'

'Yes. Digging is a job for an Elf: we are at home underground. Humans are fit only for labouring jobs.'

'Well, thanks a lot for the compliment!' said David. 'This tunnel would be a good idea, I think, if we could trust you, Elgrim. But how can we? We mean to take the Golden Cactus back to its rightful owners. You want to steal it for yourself. How *can* we work together?'

'Let us agree simply to build the tunnel together,' said Elgrim, 'for we all wish to get inside Castle Doom. But once we are through the tunnel and within the castle walls, then let the truce be ended. I shall try to get the Golden Cactus. So will you. And remember this,' said the Elf, craftily, 'Whoever gets the prize will be able to *escape* down that tunnel.'

David and Toby looked at each other.

'Think it over during the night,' said Elgrim. 'I will call an hour before dawn for your answer.'

'What! Wait all night?' said Toby. 'Don't you want to start right away?'

'I do not dig with my fingers,' retorted Elgrim. 'There is iron ore beneath our feet and I have tools to make.' He stared at Toby. 'And another weapon I must forge,' he said, 'to replace my Thuribor. This shall be a dagger, invisible to any eye, to deal death silently and unseen, and I shall call it Sohrn, which means the Victorious. Beware the vengeance of Sohrn! And now,' he said abruptly, 'I go. At dawn I come for your answer.'

'You can have our answer now,' said David, with a quick glance at Toby. 'We accept the truce.' Toby nodded and said: 'We'll be ready when you come, Elgrim.'

'Then it is agreed,' said the Elf. 'Eat well and sleep soundly. The work tomorrow will be hard.' The door slammed behind him.

David ran across the room, pulled the door ajar and peered out. But the Elf had vanished as if the earth had swallowed him up. And, as Toby said, perhaps it *had*.

As Elgrim had forecast, it was only about a couple of hours before there was the sound of trumpets on the crest of the hill to their right. A black flag with a single white diagonal stripe suddenly streamed from a pole on the topmost turret of Castle Doom to signal the arrival of the evil Baron and his men. A moment later they saw a long file of horsemen and foot soldiers weaving their way among the distant rocks.

The sun went down. The air grew chill. And, as darkness fell, bright lights beamed from the window slits of the black castle.

'I bet they're having a wonderful meal in there,' said Toby, enviously. 'Did you hear what Elgrim said? – "Eat well and sleep soundly"? We've nothing to eat, so how *can* we sleep soundly? And it's no fun sitting here in the dark,' he added crossly. 'We've not even a candle. And if we did have a candle, I'd eat it, not burn it.'

'You'd eat *half* of it,' said David. 'Don't forget, I'm as hungry as you are.'

As he spoke, the room seemed suddenly to fill with a gentle yellow light. The air grew warm. And in front of the two boys, as they squatted on the floor, there appeared – out of thin air – huge metal bowls of steaming, savoury soup.

'From Elgrim, I'll bet!' said David. And then – 'But do you think it's safe to eat?'

'He needs us to be strong for tomorrow's work,' said Toby, seizing his bowl and plunging in his spoon. 'He's not going to poison us yet. Aaaaah! This is *good*!'

As soon as the bowls were empty (and that was very quickly indeed) they vanished, to be replaced by vast platters of grilled steaks. 'Any chips?' asked Toby anxiously. And at once his plate was heaped with them.

It was indeed a most memorable meal. 'And just think of it,' murmured David, as empty plates and beakers vanished before their eyes, 'there's no washing-up!'

Toby's last words before he fell asleep were: 'I've made up my mind, David. When I leave school I'm going to learn to be a chef and I'll have a restaurant of my own. I'll be the best chef in the world. I'll be a regular Gordon Blue!'

'A what?' asked David, but the only answer he got was a loud snore, and a minute later he was sound asleep himself.

It seemed no time at all before a pounding on the door

brought them to their feet, and there stood Elgrim carrying the tools he had made during the night. He handed each of them a short, sturdy spade and a leather bag, in which to remove earth as they dug the tunnel.

'Now follow me,' said Elgrim, swinging his own spade over his shoulder. 'And remember: the truce lasts until we are all three inside Castle Doom – not a moment longer.' And he marched out leaving them to follow.

'You heard that?' David whispered to Toby as they walked out into the chill air. 'That means that as soon as we're out of the tunnel, he'll be up to something! I wonder what dirty trick he'll try to play on us then?'

'I only wish I knew!' said Toby.

CHAPTER 23

THE TALKING WALL

THE white clouds of steam were piled above the hissing, bubbling waters of the lake so that only the turrets of Castle Doom stood clear against the pale sky. Until the sun rose high, Elgrim and the boys would be safe from the prying eyes of sentries on the battlements.

At length the Elf stopped behind a large clump of bushes near the water's edge.

'We start here,' he said. 'The distance from the land to the castle is shortest at this point. In this place, too, the hot gases that keep the water boiling do not rise through the earth.'

'I hope you're right about that,' grunted Toby.

'On such matters an Elf is never wrong,' snapped Elgrim. 'Pass back the soil as I dig and spread it here. Do not pile it in a heap to catch the eye of any sentry. Now – to work!' And he plunged his spade into the earth.

He dug with fantastic speed. If you were to push your finger into a lump of soft butter, it would give you a slight idea of how Elgrim seemed to melt into the ground. David and Toby, crawling along behind him, were hard put to it to move the earth fast enough. The Elf, of course, was working standing up but David and Toby had to do their part of the task on hands and knees and, as the tunnel curved under the bed of Boiling Lake, the heat became almost unbearable. Now they were beyond all reach of any light from the entrance to the shaft but still Elgrim hewed away without pause.

'We could do with a candle,' panted David.

'No need,' said the Elf. 'I know which way I'm going. Don't waste your breath. Keep that soil moving!'

David was furious, but the middle of a tunnel under a lake was no place to argue. He pushed back a sackful of earth to Toby, who passed him an empty one and lugged the other to the tunnel entrance.

Toby's task was as hard as David's but he did have the advantage of getting a breath of fresh air now and again. He tipped out the earth behind the bushes and began to spread it. As he did so a large clod of clay slipped from the spade at his feet. Toby stooped to pick it up and throw it where he wanted it to go, and as he fumbled for it in the half darkness, he suddenly cried: 'Oooh!' Right across the inside of three fingers was a cut from which the blood was already beginning to ooze. This was amazing, for the lump of clay was . . . just a lump of clay. There were no sharp pieces of flint sticking out of it.

Toby stuffed his handkerchief into his fist and knelt to examine the piece of clay more closely. And, as he brought his other hand . . . very carefully! . . . towards it, his finger suddenly touched something, something solid, but *something his eyes could not see*!

Very, very carefully, he moved his fingers around the unseen object, tracing its shape in the sand. The shape was that of a dagger!

'Sohrn!' whispered Toby. 'It's the invisible magic dagger that Elgrim said he was going to make last night! It must have fallen from his belt while he was digging. Now what do I do? It could be very useful to David and me. But then, being a magic dagger, it might fly back to Elgrim if he calls for it. No,' Toby told himself, 'it's got to be kept out of Elgrim's hands. But how?'

There was a faint cry of 'Toby!' from the tunnel. David must have another bag of earth ready and be getting impatient. Something had to be done about Sohrn – and quickly!

Toby felt for the handle of the magic dagger. Then with a quick slash, he cut a piece from the sack that had held the soil. He wrapped the dagger in it and, running swiftly to the edge of the lake, let the package fall through the shallow water and dropped a heavy stone upon it.

'Elgrim's magic can't call you through water,' said Toby as he dashed back into the tunnel, 'and *I* know where to find you.'

After some hours the floor of the tunnel curved upwards again. Toby came crawling back from the entrance and spoke to David.

'What's that?' asked Elgrim sharply, ceasing his digging.

'He says he thinks there may be someone patrolling along the lake-side . . .' said David.

'I pulled some bushes over the mouth of our tunnel,' said Toby. 'But I think it's risky to go out again.'

'Then spread the next few bags of earth along the floor of the tunnel,' said Elgrim. 'There will not be many, for the task is nearly done.' And he struck furiously with his spade at the roof of the tunnel.

It was not long before they heard the ring of metal on stone, and Elgrim called the boys to him.

'There is a large stone slab above my head,' he said. 'I think it must be part of the floor of some room within the Castle. But all my strength is not enough to lift it. Stand beside me and push together.

The three of them heaved and strained but they managed to lift one side only a couple of inches. David whispered: 'It seems to be a room. It is very dark but I can just make out the legs of a chair or a stool.'

'Since we cannot lift the slab right up,' said Elgrim, 'let us try to slide it forward.' After a great deal of effort they managed to make an opening big enough to climb through. Elgrim was first out and as David and Toby climbed out, he held up a warning hand. They were in a grim, stone-walled room – a prison cell – with a door made of stout iron bars. A little light came through a slit window high in one wall.

'If that door's locked, we've had all our work for nothing,' said Toby. He moved forward to examine it but Elgrim waved him back.

'They would not lock the door of an empty cell,' he said. 'Stay here while I take a look down the corridor outside to find if it is safe to move further. My eyes are better than yours in this dim light.' Elgrim opened the door cautiously and slipped through, closing it behind him.

'That's silly,' said David. 'He should leave it open in case he spots a guard and has to dash back.'

'He's not being silly,' said Toby excitedly. 'He's doing it deliberately, David don't you see . . . ?'

But Toby had realised the truth too late.

As he spoke there was the jingle of a chain from the other side of the door, the grating of a key in the lock, and then the massive iron bolt shot home with a crash.

And there was Elgrim, looking in on them and sneering: 'So you thought you were a match for the wits of an Elf? What fools you are! You forgot that our bargain lasted only until we got inside Castle Doom. Well, you *are* inside – but what good can it do you? Say farewell to the Golden Cactus. I go to get it. It is mine.'

'You won't carry it out through *this* tunnel,' said David. 'Because we shall stop you.'

'I will give you one chance to save your lives, since you once saved mine,' said Elgrim. 'Go at once through the tunnel and flee – go back where you came from. For as soon as I have the Golden Cactus in my grasp, I will send Sohrn, my invisible dagger, to go before me and slay any living thing that is in the cell or in the tunnel. Flee, before your lives are forfeit!' And they heard his stealthy footsteps fade away into silence.

'And *now* what do we do?' asked David.

'Well, you can forget about Sohrn flying in and slicing your head off,' said Toby, 'because Sohrn is safely under two feet of water.' He told David about finding the magic dagger, and David felt very proud of him for being so smart – and told him so, too.

'But it doesn't help us to get out of this cell,' said Toby, moodily. 'We're certainly not going to run away now. So we'd better start thinking hard.'

Toby can always think harder when he is comfortable, so he sat on the stool and leaned back against the wall of the cell.

And out of the wall, right beside his ear, there came – *a voice.* It spoke faintly and slowly, but the words were perfectly clear.

'Friends, dear friends,' said the voice. 'Who are you, and what are you doing here?'

CHAPTER 24

COUNT OTTO'S SECRET

'DAVID! Did you hear that?' cried Toby.

'Hear what?'

'Sit here. Put your head back just like I was doing. Now: listen.'

And David, too, heard the voice.

'Can you hear me, friends?' it said. 'Please, please, speak to me.'

'It's coming from here,' said Toby. 'Look . . .'

A trickle of powdered mortar fell from between two of the great stone blocks in the wall of the cell and they could hear a faint scraping.

David put his mouth to the crack. 'The hole is nearly through,' he said. 'We will work on it from this side.' And he added: 'If Black Walter is your enemy, then we are your friends.'

The two boys went to work like mad with their pocket knives but it was nearly an hour before they had dug out a very narrow slit.

'At long last,' said the voice, 'I see a glimmer of daylight!'

'Why, isn't there a window in your cell?' asked Toby.

'No window, no door. Black Walter had me walled in here to die in darkness. Tell me if you know – did he steal the Golden Cactus from the people of Blumendorf after all?'

'He did,' said David. 'And we've come to get it back for them.'

'I, Count Otto, counselled him against such wickedness. I was a friend of his father, who was a good man. Because I set my face against Black Walter's evil ways, he sealed me in this cell. But he did not know I had a knife hidden in my clothing,' said the Count grimly. 'I have dug out the mortar round two of these great blocks. If you can work a little longer from your side I am sure we can move them enough for me to get through. And then – I promise you, I will give you what help I can in rescuing the Golden Cactus for its rightful owners.'

David and Toby worked like demons, until all the blades of their pocket-knives were worn away and the light from the tiny window faded as a cloud passed over the sun. Then, suddenly, a hefty push from Count Otto shifted one of the great blocks a few inches forward. The two boys were able to get a grip on it and between the three of them they brought it crashing to the floor. A few minutes later the second block joined it and the grey-haired Count Otto, his velvet jerkin and hose torn and covered in dust, squeezed himself through the wall and gripped their hands in gratitude.

'By all the warrior gods!' he cried, looking at the gaping hole in the floor of the cell. 'You tunnel better than the moles! Escape will be easy. Now let us go and find the Golden Cactus . . .'

'That's not so simple as you seem to think, Count Otto,' said David. 'You see, the cell door is locked.' And he told the Count all about Elgrim and his knavery.

The Count smiled. 'Let us say that it is not so *hard* as *you* seem to think,' he said. 'I planned and built this castle for Black Walter's father to be a safe retreat for him in troubled times. There are secret ways within it that I have never disclosed to his wicked son.'

'But surely there can't be a secret way out of a prison cell!' said Toby. 'That'd be a silly thing to have!'

'True,' said the Count. 'But the place where we now stand was really built as a library. It was Black Walter who burned the books and turned the place into dungeons. Look at this carving,' he went on, crossing to the opposite wall. 'Here is a rose. Here is a daffodil . . . A row of carvings, and all are flowers. All flowers except this one, which is an oak-leaf. Now, watch!' He gripped the carving and gave it a quick twist. Without a sound, a part of the solid wall swung open like a door. The boys were thrilled.

'A real secret passage!' said David.

'One of many that I know,' laughed Count Otto. 'This one runs through the wine-cellars and the kitchens – so that the master can keep an eye upon his servants – and then it runs behind the panelling of the Great Hall. That is where Black Walter will be, and where the Golden Cactus will be also – within his sight until the richest men in the world have bargained for it and the highest bidder carries it away.'

'Come on, then, and let's see what he's doing,' said David.

But Toby hung back. His jaws were working furiously and he found it difficult to speak.

'Waiwaminni!' said Toby. 'Waiwaminni!' And he ran over to the iron door of the cell.

'Is this Elf-witchery?' demanded Count Otto. 'Is there a spell upon the boy?'

'I don't think it's witchery,' David laughed. '*I* think he's got a mouthful of chewing-gum. I think he meant to say "*Wait a minute*".'

'Yes, that's what it was,' said Toby, speaking clearly this time. 'I'm stuffing the lock on this door full of chewing-gum and bits of mortar. Elgrim locked us in – but when he tries to escape this way he'll find what he really did was to lock himself *out*.'

'I pity the Elf who matches his wits against that boy,' said Count Otto and David added: 'Good for you, Toby. You've really gummed up the works!'

The secret door swung shut behind them and they followed Count Otto along the narrow passage, lit by narrow slits in the outer wall of the castle. They looked down through holes cunningly disguised among carvings and saw the servants filling great flagons from the enormous barrels in the wine-cellar. They looked down into the vast kitchen where the carcases of wild boars turned on their spits over huge fires and hordes of cooks, assistant-cooks and servants scurried about like ants.

Toby took deep breaths of the savoury air. Then he said: 'I can't bear it any longer. Let's move on.' It's a terrible feeling, to be so near to such a lot of food when you're as hungry as he was.

They heard the noise of revelry from the Great Hall of Castle Doom long before the secret passage reached it and when at length they looked down through the cunningly hidden spy-holes they realised what an impossible task it was that faced them. This is what they saw:

The torch-lit Great Hall – with its heavily-beamed ceiling, and its panelled walls hung with paintings of fierce warriors, with coats of arms, shields, maces, spears and every imaginable kind of weapon – was packed with the Baron's black-tattooed horde of cut-throats. They lolled at long oaken tables, toasting each other in great goblets of wine and gnawing on the meat-bones that they gripped in their massive fists. At the far end of the hall carpenters were just finishing the building of a small platform.

But it was what they saw just a few feet below them, close to the wall behind which their secret passage ran, that set David and Toby tingling with the thrill of danger. For they looked down on the tattooed head of Black Walter himself, sitting at a table alone and leaning back against the panelling of their hide-out while he looked on the merry-making of his men and, from time to time, leafed through the well-worn pages of a big book.

And, on another table set near the evil Baron, stood the stolen cactus, secure in its padlocked cage and giving out its golden radiance.

As they looked in breathless wonder, Black Walter

suddenly rose and banged on the table with his sword. Silence fell at once.

'To continue our celebration of the seizure of the Golden Cactus, which will make every man among us wealthy,' he said, to a burst of cheers, 'I am about to present a very entertaining spectacle. You all know that I keep a Torture Book' (nobody cheered at this). 'Well, I am going to show you Torture Number 129b. It is most ingenious and I want every member of my household to see and enjoy it.'

'And afterwards, my bold warriors,' added Black Walter, 'I will broach the only cask that remains of the treasure of Castle Doom, the Wine of the Sword – the wine of warriors, the noblest drink in the world!'

And amid the wild cheers of the roysterers, Black Walter signalled for the victim to be brought in to suffer Torture Number 129b.

CHAPTER 25

BLACK WALTER MEETS HIS MATCH

DAVID said: 'Does Black Walter really mean to call all his servants in to watch the torture?'

'Every one of them,' answered Count Otto. 'He likes to show them what can happen to *them* if he is disobeyed.'

'Then the kitchens and the wine-cellar will be empty. And that gives me an idea,' said David, excitedly. 'Toby, have you still got your Shaggy Dog stone? Put it on the stone floor here with mine.' And when Toby did so, David began to stamp on the two stones.

'What are you trying to do?' asked Count Otto.

'I'm trying to break the stones down to a powder,' said David, panting, 'but it's harder than I thought.'

'Then let me try,' said the Count. 'I am heavier than you and my boots are shod with iron. There,' he went on, stamping away, 'I have ground them into powder for you, though I cannot see how this will help us get the

Golden Cactus away from Black Walter.'

'There isn't time to explain,' said David. 'Please trust me. I want you to do something. It *will* help us to get the Golden Cactus, I'm sure.'

'Then tell me and it shall be done,' said Count Otto.

'You can get into the wine-cellar?' The Count nodded. 'And you know which cask holds the Wine of the Sword?'

'No difficulty there,' laughed the Count. 'I know it well – I was present when it was filled, some years ago.'

'Then please, go quickly and put all this powder into the cask,' said David, scooping it into his handkerchief and handing it to the Count.

Toby, all this time, had had his eyes glued to the spy-holes and as the Count strode off down the secret passage, he called:

'David! Come quickly and see what they're doing.'

David joined him and saw that on the platform at the far end of the Great Hall an enormous glass tank had been set up and half filled with water. The hall was now packed with Black Walter's household staff standing round the walls and in the spaces between the long tables. Suddenly two burly torturers, stripped to the waist and with black masks covering their eyes, pushed their way through the crowd around the door, dragging their victim towards the tank.

'It's Elgrim!' cried Toby.

And Elgrim it was. The Elf's hands were tied behind his back, but although he must have realised that death was near, there was no fear in his face – only a great fury.

David said: 'Look at him, Toby! I'm sure he has some scheme in his mind. It's late in the afternoon so it won't be very long before his magic power starts coming back to him.'

The wicked Baron had made his way to the end of the Hall and now he spoke almost as if he knew what David had said.

'A rope round the Elf – quickly. Throw it over that beam and lift him from the ground . . . an Elf with his feet off the ground can draw no magic from the spirits of the earth. Now lower him into the tank. Elves also cannot swim,' said Black Walter, while the torturers lowered Elgrim until the water came to his shoulders.

'It is this fact that makes Torture Number 129b so amusing, as you will see. Look upon this traitor, who tired to steal the Golden Cactus from us,' he added amid a roar of angry voices. 'This is the robber who left a message for me that said: "*You fool, Black Walter – The Golden Cactus is mine*!" Well, who is the fool, now?'

As he learned how David had altered his message, the Elf cried out in anger: '*I* did not write that you were a fool. Let me go and I will guide you to the one who did. He is in the Castle at this very moment. He is in . . .'

Elgrim was going to say that David was locked up in one of the dungeons, but he never got so far. With a gesture of contempt, Black Walter gave a signal to the torturers and Elgrim was dropped under the water.

He was pulled up again, spluttering, and this time there was real fear on his face.

'It is too late for excuses,' said the Baron, 'so save your breath – you will need it.' He signalled to the torturers to fasten the rope so that Elgrim was once more head and shoulders above the water. Then he revealed the full horror of Torture Number 129b.

'We will drink to the death of Elgrim the Traitor,' said Black Walter. 'Fill your goblets and file past the tank. And let every man, when he has drunk destruction to the Elf, pour a little of his wine into the tank. As the level rises the Elf must either drink or drown.' A roar of coarse laughter went up from the black warriors as he added: 'And when he can no longer drink he will most certainly drown!'

Chanting and shouting the warriors filed past the tank, leering at the doomed Elf as little by little the level of water and wine rose to his chin. Only the evil mind of Black Walter could have thought out such a torture. It was a particularly terrible one to Elgrim because, as everybody knows, Elves live mostly underground and therefore never drink anything except root beer. They hate wine as much as boys and girls hate medicine.

'I don't like Elgrim,' muttered Toby, 'but I don't like to see this happening to him.'

'Wait until my plan starts to work,' said David. 'He'll get his chance to escape.' Just then Count Otto touched him on the shoulder and whispered: 'I've put the powder in the wine – and I was just in time. Already the cask is being hauled up to the Great Hall.'

'And now,' said David, 'is there any opening in this passage from which we can reach the Golden Cactus?'

'There is a small panel here that slides back,' said the Count. 'It is some feet above the cactus. But if you climb down it will be difficult to get back. And the opening is not big enough to take the case in which the cactus is locked.'

'I think I can see a way round all the difficulties,' said David. And he began to outline his plan.

Now the great cask containing the famous Wine of the Sword was rolled in and set up on trestles. Warriors and servants passed before it, filling their goblets with the potent drink.

When all were filled, Black Walter raised his own goblet and cried: 'A toast to the Golden Cactus and the wealth it will bring to us!' Amid the laughter and shouts of the roysterers he strode over to Elgrim and dashed the dregs of his wine into the face of the Elf. 'A last drink before you drown,' he snarled.

'Now's our chance,' said David.

Count Otto slid back the panel and down towards the Golden Cactus went David – head first, while Toby and the Count hung on to his heels. In seconds the wooden keys that he had carved had opened the locks. He whipped off the cage and the glass cover. The bowl in which the Golden Cactus grew and shone was in his hands.

'Hoist away!' he yelled.

And at that moment Black Walter, turning to go back to his seat, saw what was happening. With a cry of anger he drew his sword and leaped towards David. But even as he sprang his cry turned to a yell of fear . . . a yell that was repeated from every throat in the Great Hall.

This is David's moment of triumph—a double triumph, because not only has he got the Golden Cactus in his grasp, but Black Walter has suddenly grown so enormous that he's jammed firmly against the ceiling of his castle hall and can't get at David with his sword. The marvellous power of the Shaggy Dog stones was something of which the Villain was completely ignorant—probably because nobody had ever dared to tell him a Shaggy Dog story.

For suddenly Black Walter and his wicked followers found the Great Hall shrinking around them as they grew . . . and . . . *grew* . . . and *GREW*! Burly six-foot soldiers shot up suddenly to four times their normal height. Skulls cracked agonisingly against the beams of the ceiling and the Great Hall, which had seemed full of people before, was now packed solid with terrified giants forced down on all fours and fighting each other madly as they sought to escape through a door that was now too low and too narrow for them to pass through.

'The Shaggy Dog stones!' gloated Toby as he and Count Otto hauled David back into the secret passage. 'They worked, David! They worked! Black Walter and his men can't get out of the hall! We can take it easy now. Let's stop at the kitchens on our way out and have something to eat.'

But David was cautious. 'We don't know how long the effects of the stones will last,' he said. 'Let's get out of Castle Doom as fast as we can.'

So, with the light of the Golden Cactus to ease their way, they set off for the escape tunnel while David explained to the baffled Count Otto the secret of the Shaggy Dog stones.

Soon they were back in the cell. David whipped off his jerkin and carefully wrapped the Golden Cactus in it.

'Good-bye, Castle Doom! Good-bye, Black Walter!' Toby laughed as they stepped towards the entrance to the tunnel.

A cry of fury interrupted him. They all swung round.

There outside the cell, shaking the iron door and snarling like a mad dog was Elgrim the Elf . . . *but an Elgrim now eight feet tall and with a terrible strength in his great muscular arms.*

'Quick! Into the tunnel!' shouted David.

In Elgrim's enormous hands the stout bars began to bend – and, before the three companions were half-way through the tunnel, the earth beneath them shuddered as the iron door crashed to the ground. Elgrim was at their heels.

CHAPTER 26

THE END OF CASTLE DOOM

DAVID went first along the tunnel with the Golden Cactus, followed by Toby and Count Otto. Fear gave them speed and soon they crawled out into the fading daylight.

From the darkness of the tunnel they could hear the ring of Elgrim's spade and the curses of the maddened Elf as he widened the passage – for he was now four times as big as when he dug his way in – and shovelled the earth behind him.

'What about blocking up this end of the tunnel?' suggested Count Otto.

'It wouldn't keep Elgrim back,' said Toby. 'The Shaggy Dog stones made him bigger and stronger. That's how he was able to escape. But I'm wondering if they've done something else – if they've made his magic powers stronger, too? The sun is sinking and his magic will soon return.'

'Then there's no time to waste,' cried the Count. 'We must run and hide – at least until daylight, when the Elf magic will have died away.'

'No. Once he gets out of that tunnel we're finished,' said David. 'We've got to deal with Elgrim *now*, in some way. But how? Think! We must all think – quickly!'

Toby said after a moment: 'What about Sohrn – Elgrim's magic-dagger? Could we use that?'

'I think it's safer under the water, where you dropped it,' said David. 'Suppose you fished it out and Elgrim happened to call for it. It might leave your hand and fly back to him. And then,' added David, 'we *would* be in a mess.'

'Fly back to him?' said Toby thoughtfully. 'Fly back to him? Why, that's it! That's the idea! We'll *send* it back to him! I'm going to get Sohrn out of the water.' He broke off a long branch from one of the bushes by the tunnel mouth and ran down to the lake.

Elgrim was more than half-way along the tunnel by now and they could clearly hear his angry growls as he shovelled away at a furious pace.

Count Otto was baffled. 'A magic dagger that belongs to the evil Elf . . . and you would give it back to him?' he said. 'I do not understand.'

'Neither do I – yet,' said David. 'But whatever Toby has in mind I'll bet it won't do Elgrim any good!'

Toby came running up. He took Count Otto's hand and placed something in his palm. The Count jumped.

'I see nothing,' he declared, 'but I feel the handle of a dagger.' Gingerly he moved the other hand towards it. And now I feel the blade. What would you have me do?'

'I want you to stand astride the entrance to the tunnel,' said Toby, '— like that. Good. You are stronger than we are, Count Otto, and you have a long arm. I want you to face the Castle and, when I say so, fling Sohrn as high into the air as you can . . . right over the top of the tunnel.'

The Count placed himself in position while Toby squatted near the entrance of the tunnel.

'Now!' said Toby.

The Count hurled the magic dagger high into the air with all his force and, just as Toby felt it must have gone as high as it could, he shouted: 'Oh Sohrn, Sohrn, invisible dagger of Elgrim the Elf, return to your master!'

At his cry the digging inside the tunnel stopped suddenly. Outside, the invisible dagger came screaming down at magical speed. All that the watchers on the shore could see was a sudden spurt of water.

Then from Elgrim's throat there came a screech of terror.

'No! No! Sohrn – go back! Go back!'

But the Elf saw his danger too late. For, as soon as the heavy, speeding dagger clove through the water, Elgrim's magic became powerless to command it. Sohrn the invisible, the victorious, returned to its maker. It pierced the roof of the tunnel as if it had been made of paper and the seething waters of Boiling Lake followed it, widening the hole until, suddenly, the entire tunnel caved in and buried the evil Elf forever.

The three watchers stood in silence, staggered by the swiftness with which the thing had happened.

At last Count Otto spoke. 'An invisible dagger, to strike men down unseen,' he said. 'It was an evil thing and now it has slain the evil one who made it. But there is other evil to be destroyed and it is my duty to carry out the sentence of death. There is no time to lose.'

He strode off in the direction of the ruined tower, with David and Toby hurrying to keep pace with him and asking him to tell them what was in his mind.

Count Otto, however, would say nothing until they reached the ruined tower. Then he said: 'I fear the effects of that strange stone will wear off. Black Walter and his terrible warriors will become their normal size. Then once again they will march from Castle Doom to rob and plunder. That must never happen. Wait in the tower here for my return. I shall not be long.'

'But can't we help you?' said David and Toby together.

'One pair of hands will be enough,' said Count Otto, grimly. 'When I built Castle Doom I made certain that if ever an attacker managed to get into the Castle he would never leave it. The key to my secret weapon is hidden among the rocks not far from this tower. Watch the turrets of Castle Doom and you shall see justice done upon Black Walter.'

Count Otto vanished among the piles of rocks while David and Toby pushed open the door of the ruined tower. David put the Golden Cactus on the floor and opened its covering to give it air. Its golden radiance flooded the room as they went across to the window that looked over Boiling Lake.

Before them Castle Doom stood out, black and evil, amid the white clouds that rose from the seething, moonlit waters.

And suddenly, as they watched wonderingly, the great black mass of the Castle, and the craggy rocks on which it stood, split in two from top to bottom. A soaring mass of yellow flame shot into the sky and a moment later the ruined tower rocked to the crash of a shattering explosion.

'He's blown up the arsenal under the Castle!' cried David.

'Look! Look!' said Toby.

The violence of the explosion must have broken a way through the bed of the lake to the sleeping volcano below. For, with a shuddering, rending crash, an earthquake split the entire valley from end to end and Castle Doom, with all the waters of Boiling Lake, plunged from sight into the bowels of the earth.

And as David and Toby stood, aghast and speechless at the sight, a harsh voice spoke from behind them.

'Traitors! Robbers!' it said. 'Here is one, faithful to his trust, who will avenge his master, Black Walter!'

There, advancing on them with drawn sword as they turned, was a tall figure in black chain-mail.

It was Sandor . . . the last of the black warriors.

CHAPTER 27

MR STRRETCH TELLS HIS SECRET

TOBY said: 'How can we be robbers, Sandor? We are returning the Golden Cactus to the poor villagers who are its rightful owners. Surely you know that Black Walter stole the cactus?'

'I know,' said Sandor. 'And I know that the Baron did other evil things. But when my master died and I was hungry, Black Walter took me into his service. His enemies are mine – even you, who saved my life. So you must die.'

There was no escape. The great sword flashed as Sandor raised his arm to strike them down – just as Count Otto stepped through the open door.

The sound made Sandor swing round, his sword held high. But at the sight of the Count his weapon clattered to the floor and the black warrior cowered back against the wall, a hand across his eyes.

'A ghost!' he whispered in terror.

'I am no ghost, Sandor,' said Count Otto, gripping the man's wrist and pulling his hand away. 'Do ghosts grip like this? Is their touch warm on your skin? Look at me!'

Slowly the warrior opened his eyes.

'Count Otto!' he gasped, '— and alive! But . . .'

'But Black Walter told you I was dead,' said the Count. 'I was walled up in one of his dungeons – until these boys set me free. So, you see, Black Walter tricked you into working for him. You owe him no loyalty. In fact,' said the Count with a smile, 'since I am still alive, I consider you are still in my service.'

'So everybody's happy!' said Toby. 'Now we can get on with the job of taking the Golden Cactus back to Blumendorf.'

Count Otto, of course, wanted them to go to his castle and meet all his family but the boys pointed out that they had pledged themselves to restore the Golden Cactus. 'Duty comes first,' said the Count. 'One day in the future, however, I trust you will return.'

Sandor offered them his horse but David took him on one side and pointed out that the Count must be very weary after him imprisonment and in need of rest.

So in the end David and Toby waved farewell as the great black horse bore their friends back to their home.

'And now, which road shall we take back to Uncle Septimus and Blumendorf?' asked David, carefully folding his jerkin round the Golden Cactus.

'Let's go by the track I came on,' said Toby. 'I know a place on the way where there's lots and lots of lovely wild raspberries.'

'You *would*!' laughed David.

Despite a very long stop for what Toby called his 'fruit lunch', they made very good time (there being now no Elgrim or black warriors about to hinder them) and before sunset they crossed the river by a ford within sight of the House of Cobwebb.

'I think we ought to tidy ourselves up before we meet Uncle Septimus,' said David, putting down his burden. So they knelt by the water and washed their hands and faces and wet their hair and smoothed it down and climbed up the river bank again feeling very much refreshed.

'But you still look scruffy without your jerkin,' said Toby.

'Oh, I'm going to put it on now,' David told him. 'I'm going to hold my hands out in front and carry the Golden Cactus so they'll all see its light as we get near the house and come running out.' And he bent down to open his jerkin and take out the Golden Cactus.

And . . . *it just wasn't there*!

Frantically they ran about, searching among the bushes, until finally David said: 'This is silly. If it was anywhere within sight we should see the light from it.'

'You don't think there's *another* Elf like that awful Elgrim, do you?' said Toby, wearily.

'I don't know. I think it's terrible going back without the Golden Cactus, but we've got to seek help. Let's get to Uncle Septimus as quickly as we can tell him what's happened.'

The grounds of the great house were deserted. There was no sight nor sound of life. The boys panted up the long drive. The huge door gaped open. They ran in, calling frantically: 'Uncle Septimus! Uncle Septimus! Where are you?'

'Here,' came the answer, in Captain Cobwebb's deep voice. 'In the banqueting room.'

They raced along the corridor and came into the vast central room of the house crying: 'We defeated Black Walter and Elgrim too and we got the Golden Cactus and we were nearly here when . . .'

And then they stopped.

In the middle of the room, in the centre of the enormous dining table there stood, in a blaze of light, the Golden Cactus!

A great roar of 'Welcome back!' went up from all

their friends of the House of Cobwebb who thronged the room, then silence fell as Captain Cobwebb spoke.

'We knew you had recovered the Golden Cactus, boys,' he said. 'We saw you as you approached the house. We saw who robbed you of your prize. Tell them the name of the thief, Mr Strretch.'

Mr Strretch stepped forward, placed his cane under one arm, carefully removed his white gloves, and gave a little cough. From the top of his tall hat the Oookuk poked its head out and regarded the two boys with a beady eye.

Mr Strretch lifted one hand, finger outstretched.

'There, me noble warriors,' he said, '*there* is the culprit – this featherbrained, flapping egg-collector,' – and he pointed to the Oookuk. 'Ever since it thought it had hatched me out of an egg,' declared Mr Strretch, 'it's been trying to find an egg that would hatch out *another* outsize chick. Some days ago it dropped a melon on me hat. Yesterday it staggered home in great joy and struck me down with an ancient cannon-ball. An hour ago, however, it came winging home with the Golden Cactus. So, me brave companions, all's well that end's well!'

Captain Cobwebb broke in. 'We are proud of you, boys,' he said, 'and tomorrow you shall return the Golden Cactus to the people of Blumendorf. But now you need food and sleep. Don't keep them talking too long, Mr Strretch.'

Toby said: 'What beats me about that bird's flying off with the Golden Cactus is why we never heard it crying "*oookuk . . . oookuk*" like it usually does. We didn't hear a sound at all.'

'Ah, that's just another oddity about this feathered freak,' declared Mr Strretch. 'You know that when Spring is over ordinary cuckoos can't say "cuckoo" at all – they just make a sort of croak. But the Oookuk won't do anything that *they* do. It loses its voice altogether. That's why you heard nothing.'

David said: 'Aren't you worried, Mr Strretch, about what the Oookuk may drop on your hat next?'

'Not a bit, me worthy friend!' declared Mr Strretch. 'By the exercise of the human intellect I have ensured that this bird will be no future trouble to me at all. An hour ago I took a hen's egg, covered it in gold paint, and presented it to the creature. Now it sits happily and contentedly upon it, waiting for it to hatch.'

'But when it *has* hatched,' Toby asked, 'what then?'

Mr Strretch leaned over the two boys, put his arm round their shoulders and drew their heads very close to his.

'Don't let it hear this,' he whispered, 'but, me noble companions, have you ever heard of any bird hatching a *hard-boiled* egg?'

CHAPTER 28

WHAT A DAY THAT WAS!

YOU can be sure that David and Toby will never in all their lives forget their triumphal entry into Blumendorf next day. Mr Mysto produced out of thin air a magnificent open coach and four white horses to draw it and they took their seats. On a platform behind them – raised up so that all the onlookers along the route could see it – the Golden Cactus seemed to dim the sunlight with its brilliant rays.

Mr Muscle, in a cocked hat, scarlet coat and silken knee-breeches, leaped into the coachman's seat, cracked his long whip and amid the cheers of all their friends, led by Mr Strretch, they set off at a spanking pace.

Even the country roads on the way to Blumendorf were lined by cheering people but the cobbled streets of the village itself were packed tight, for farming folk had come to the celebrations from miles around.

The Mayor and Councillors met the coach as Mr Muscle reined up outside the old, gabled Council Hall, and there were speeches and speeches . . . and speeches . . . and handclasps . . . and embraces (David finally worked it out that he had had his hand shaken eight hundred times and had been kissed on both cheeks by fifteen councillors, the village constable, the local tax-collector and a man with a big brush whose job was to keep the streets clean.)

Then David and Toby handed over the Golden Cactus and the Mayor carried it into the Council Chamber where it was reverently placed on a silken cloth in the middle of the big round table. And then the Mayor led them into the banqueting room, leaving villagers and visitors to file in their hundreds through the Council Chamber, marvelling at the Golden Cactus and telling each other how rich the village would be after all the millionaires in the world had come to bid against each other for its shining blooms.

There really isn't space or time to tell you all about that lunch that David and Toby had with the Mayor and the elders of Blumendorf. I'll just remind you that these were country-folk (and mainly farmers at that), and that when it comes to eating, such people have no time for tiny little helpings of this-and-that with fancy names.

They were surprised and delighted to see what a couple of hungry boys could eat. David managed so many lark-ham-and-mushroom pies that the cook had to bake a second batch. And when Toby started on his twelfth plate of wild boar and chestnut purée, the Mayor rose from his seat and declared amid wild cheering that in addition to the Freedom of Blumendorf (which they'd already received) both boys would be accorded the very special honour of *rumblerumblerumblerumble*!*

Rumblerumblerumblerumble is what the words sounded like to David and Toby and they asked the Mayor very kindly to explain what he had said.

'Aha! How you will enjoy it!' said the Mayor. 'In your language you would call it the Blumendorf Blanket Sky-trip. Everybody in Blumendorf will join in to confer this supreme honour upon you.'

'Well, if a blanket sky-trip has anything to do with going to sleep, I'll be glad to take it after a lunch like this,' said Toby happily and David said: 'Me too. When do we take this blanket trip, Mr Mayor sir?'

* What the Mayor actually said, in his own language, was 'Blumendorfer wollene Bettdecke Himmelreise'. No other village anywhere has such a ceremony as this.

'Later, later,' said the Mayor. 'First we go to show you our village sports.'

After three hours of presenting prizes in the various competitions on the sports field, David whispered to Toby: 'It's jolly hard work being a distinguished visitor, isn't it?' and Toby heartily agreed. They'd seen archery competitions, crossbow competitions, tossing the tree-trunk, catching the greasy pig, eating-jelly-with-knitting-needles competitions and dozens more. But they plodded bravely on, as distinguished visitors are expected to do.

Darkness was falling before the Mayor called for the sports field to be cleared and soon the boys heard the blare of trumpets from far down the village street, and the village band came into sight, followed by the famous Blumendorf Blanket.

It was in a huge roll, hundreds of yards long and was carried on the shoulders of all the villagers. When it was laid out before the Mayor and his guests it formed a huge circle that almost covered the big sports field.

The villagers formed up around its edge and cheered their guests to the echo. Toby and David looked at the blanket. It was beautifully soft and thick and its colour was a cosy red.

'Oh, how I want to lie down and sleep and sleep!' murmured Toby.

'But please, yes, do lie down,' urged the Mayor. 'That is just how the ceremony begins.'

So they walked out to the middle of the blanket, amid much clapping, and they lay down. 'I only hope,' said David, sleepily, 'that they're going to roll us up in this and carry us back to Uncle Septimus' place.'

'Mmmm,' murmured Toby, curling up happily.

Carefully, each of the villagers gripped the edge of the blanket in both hands and the Blumendorf Blanket Skytrip began. Like this: –

With a great yell everybody round the edge of the vast blanket leaned back and pulled . . . hard. The blanket tightened. David and Toby shot high into the air and, as they came tumbling down, the taut blanket boomed like a gun and sent them higher . . . and again higher . . . and again.

It was no good shouting for help or expecting the villagers to stop because they yelled so loudly every time they jerked the boys into the air that no protests could have been heard.

'Oooooh!' cried David.

'Oooooh!' squealed Toby.

Higher and still higher they bounced.

They went into a dense black cloud . . . through it . . . out on the other side into brilliant moonlight which lit the cloud as they fell towards it again and made it look like an enormous bed of cotton wool.

Down and down the two boys tumbled. The white cloud wrapped itself around them and seemed to hold them – gently, firmly, safely.

A sudden rattling noise made them open their eyes cautiously . . .

'Wake up, boys,' said Mrs Green as she walked into their bedroom carrying a tray. 'I've brought you some supper, after all. My new washing-machine is not damaged in the least and your father says you are forgiven for putting the cups and saucers into it.'

She put the tray down.

'You know it was a most *surprising* thing!' said Mrs Green. 'A man from the electricity company came to the door not long after you had been sent to bed. He said he'd come to see if the new machine was working all right. Wasn't that fortunate! Your father told him what you'd been up to, so he made a very special examination and he found nothing wrong at all.

'He said we ought not to blame you for putting cups and saucers in it – the electricity people ought to have labelled it: *Clothes*-Washing Machine, not just *Washing*-Machine, and he is going to see that they replace all the things that were broken.'

'Oh, good,' said David, still half-awake, and Toby just grunted.

'He was such an amusing man,' smiled Mrs Green as

she went out of the bedroom. 'I wonder where he comes from? I've never met anyone around here with the name of Strretch.'